The Last Resort

Also by Tom Milton

The Godmother
Eden Valley
The Silver Locket
Orphans of War
Invisible Wounds
Leave of Absence
Outside the Gate
The Golden Door
Sara's Laughter
A Shower of Roses
Infamy
All the Flowers
The Admiral's Daughter
No Way to Peace

The Last Resort

Tom Milton

NEPPERHAN PRESS, LLC
YONKERS, NY

Published by Nepperhan Press, LLC
P.O. Box 1448, Yonkers, NY 10702
nepperhan@optonline.net
nepperhan.com

PUBLISHER'S NOTE
This is a work of fiction. Names, characters, places, and incidents
are the product of the author's imagination or are used fictitiously,
and any resemblance to actual persons, living or dead, events, or
locales is entirely coincidental.

Printed in the United States of America

Library of Congress Control Number: 2018912671

ISBN 978-1-7320634-2-6

Cover art was licensed from Publitek, Inc.

For Marie

Racism is the last resort for people who have failed to build a truly human identity.

From a student paper

No one is born hating another person because of the color of his skin. If they can learn to hate, they can be taught to love, for love comes more naturally to the human heart than its opposite.

Nelson Mandela

New York, 2017

ONE

A GUY WEARING a red baseball cap was standing across the street from her, holding a sign that said MAKE AMERICA WHITE AGAIN and staring at her with a look of hatred. It aroused a feeling that Elsa thought she had gotten over a long time ago, and though she didn't show it, she reciprocated his hatred, contradicting her sign that said LOVE WILL PREVAIL.

At that moment a shot rang out and people to her right screamed. As she turned to see what had happened she heard a metallic clunk on the street, and turning back, she saw a gun lying on the pavement in front of the guy.

When he stooped and picked it up she somehow knew he didn't intend to use it, he only wanted to prevent anyone else from using it, but suddenly from behind him a cop grabbed his arm and made him drop the gun while another cop put him into a chokehold. A third cop moved deliberately to collect the gun in a plastic bag.

It didn't take them long to haul the guy away, clearing a path through the crowd while other cops attended to someone who had evidently been hit by the shot.

"Are you okay?" Sister Solana asked her, rushing over from where she had been standing with the core of their group.

"Yeah, I'm okay," Elsa said, catching her breath.

"Did you see what happened?"

"No. I only saw the guy across from me pick up a gun, but he didn't fire it. Someone else fired it and threw it on the street in front of him."

"Well, don't move," the sister told her. "I'll be right back."

Sister Solana made her way toward the ring of cops where people had screamed. She stood back while a team of paramedics arrived with a stretcher. Elsa prayed that whoever had been hit, it wasn't a serious injury.

As she waited for the sister to return, the cop who had made the guy drop the gun approached her and asked: "Did you see what that guy did?"

"Yeah. I saw him pick up the gun."

"Did you see him fire it?"

"He didn't fire it. Whoever fired it threw it on the street in front of him."

"Are you sure?" the cop said skeptically.

"I'm positive. We were staring at each other across the street, and I didn't take my eyes off him for even a second."

The cop, who looked about her age, took out a pad and pen and asked: "What's your name?"

"Elsa Romero."

"Which group are you with today?"

"Students for Peace and Justice at St. Catherine College."

"Are you a student?"

"No, I'm a professor."

The cop looked at her as if he didn't believe she was old enough to be a professor. "Can I see your driver's license?"

She got her wallet out of her pocketbook and removed her license and handed it to him, feeling as if she had been pulled over for a traffic violation.

"So you're twenty-eight, and you live in Yonkers," the cop said, looking at her license. "Are you the leader of your group?"

"No. Sister Solana is our leader."

"Why are you here?"

"To protest against the government's immigration policies."

The cop nodded as if he understood. He looked Irish, so it had been a long time since his people were persecuted as immigrants, but he may have heard family stories about it. "Will you go with me to the precinct and make a statement? On the face of things, it looks like we caught that guy red-handed, so your statement would be helpful to him."

"Of course I will," Elsa said without hesitation. "I just need to let the sister know I won't be going back with her."

"Where is she?"

"She's over there."

After rolling up her sign she went with the cop toward the paramedics who were carrying someone on their stretcher, gliding rapidly toward the ambulance that had parted the crowd. They met Sister Solana returning from that area.

"It's a high school student from a group like ours," the sister said sadly. "The bullet hit her in the head."

"Oh, my God," Elsa said. "Did it kill her?"

"No, but it could kill her. We have to pray for her."

"Sister," the cop said respectfully, "I've asked Ms. Romero to go with me to the precinct and make a statement. She says the guy we caught didn't fire the gun."

"Yes, go with him," the sister told her. "You have my blessing. I have to round up our students and get them out of here."

"That's a good idea," the cop said.

"I'll let you know when I get home," Elsa said before going with the cop.

They walked in silence to Madison Avenue, where another cop was waiting with a car. The cop she was with politely opened the back door, made sure that she was settled, closed the door, got into the passenger seat, and explained to his partner: "We need to take her to the precinct so she can make a statement."

Unable to follow their conversation, Elsa sat back and prayed for the wounded girl and prepared herself for making a statement. She recalled clearly the way the guy had stared at her—it was a look of cold hatred, a look that could have killed. But it hadn't killed her, and the guy hadn't fired the gun that might have killed that poor girl. He had picked up the gun as if he wanted to prevent anyone else from using it. Though she couldn't be sure that this was his reason for picking up the gun, it was the only reason she could imagine that would have justified the risk of getting caught with the gun in his hand.

The car turned right and went to Third Avenue, where it turned left and went to 67th Street, where it turned left and finally stopped. The cop let her out of the car and led her up the steps of an old building with gray stone facing on the first story and brick facing on the upper stories, with arches over the windows.

Inside, after checking at a desk, the cop put her in an interview room, where he asked her to wait, telling her that a detective would be with her in a few minutes.

It was a lot longer than a few minutes, and while she waited Elsa couldn't help becoming anxious. With all the things that the government was doing to persecute immigrants, she began to wonder if they could deport her because she was born in the Dominican Republic. But she was a U.S. citizen, and she had never committed a crime, so there wasn't any reason for deporting her. Was there?

Finally, a man who looked about her father's age came into the room, saying: "I'm sorry I kept you waiting, Dr. Romero."

"That's okay," she said, realizing they had checked her out and among other things had learned that she had a doctoral degree.

"I'm Detective Ferraro," the man said, extending a hand to shake hers. In his dark eyes was the worldly sadness of a man who had seen almost everything. "I really appreciate your coming here to make a statement."

"It's not a problem."

The detective sat down at the table opposite her and reached toward a device. "I'd like to record our conversation. Is that okay?"

"Yeah, it's okay."

After turning on the device the detective leaned toward her and said: "So you're a professor at St. Catherine. You know, I got my degree in criminal justice there. It was a long time ago, but did you know Sister Audrey?"

"Yeah. I took a psychology course with her."

"A remarkable woman. She understood long before other educators that a criminal justice program belongs in a school of social and behavioral sciences."

"I wish I'd had more time with her."

"I heard she passed away."

"Yeah. It was a great loss for the college."

The detective observed a moment of silence, and then he said: "So you were demonstrating with a group called Students for Peace and Justice. Is that Pax Christi?"

"It's modeled after Pax Christi, and we support their events."

"It looks like every group was there today, including the one that caused the trouble."

"Who were those guys?"

"They were a white nationalist group. In fact, they were one of several white nationalist groups who got together for this event."

"The guy you have in custody was holding a sign that said MAKE AMERICA WHITE AGAIN."

The detective sighed. "My family were immigrants who came to this country early in the last century. They came from southern Italy, and to some people they didn't look white. When I was a kid, a teacher asked me what I wanted to be when I grew up, and you know what I said?"

"What did you say?"

"I said I wanted to be a white man."

As someone who didn't know the meaning of white until she came to America, she was touched by this admission. "So you understand."

"Yeah, I understand." The detective paused. "Now, tell me what you saw that guy do."

"I saw him standing across the street from me, holding his sign and staring at me with a look of hatred. And then, suddenly, there was a shot."

"Did that guy fire it?"

"No. He didn't."

"Are you absolutely sure?"

"Yes. I didn't take my eyes off him for even a second."

"Okay. And then what happened?"

"I heard screams from the people to my right, and I turned to see what had happened, but at that moment I heard a clunk, and I turned back and saw a gun lying on the pavement."

"How do you think the gun got there?"

"Whoever fired it must have thrown it over the heads of people in front of him."

"You're assuming it was a male."

"It's always a male, isn't it?"

The detective nodded grimly. "Now, where exactly was the gun on the pavement?"

"A few feet in front of the guy."

"And what did he do?"

"He picked it up."

"Were you afraid he was going to use it?"

"No, not at all. I thought he picked it up to prevent anyone else from using it."

"What made you think that?"

"I don't know. I guess the way he did it. And also," she remembered now, "the look in his eyes was different then."

"How was it different?"

"It wasn't a look of hatred anymore. It was a look of concern."

"So what happened next?"

"A cop, I mean a police officer, grabbed his arm from behind and made him drop the gun, and another officer put him into a chokehold."

"Okay," the detective said. "If I have this typed up, will you sign it?"

"Of course. Will you release him?"

"Well, it's not a crime to pick up a gun unless you intend to use it, and you say he didn't. But we don't know that, we're only going on your feeling about his intention. So we could hold him and try to get him to tell us who fired the gun."

"What if he doesn't know who fired it?"

"Then we won't get anything out of him. But if he was a member of that group, he might have an idea who fired it."

"Okay. Should I wait here?"

"Yeah, it won't take long to type your statement. Would you like some coffee?'

"No, thanks. But I could use some water."

Not long after the detective left the room a young woman in uniform brought her a bottle of water.

As she waited for the detective to return with the statement, Elsa was no longer anxious about herself. Instead, she was anxious about the guy. She understood why the detective wanted to hold him and question him further, but if he wasn't being charged with anything, could they still hold him? From what she knew about the criminal justice system, she didn't think they could hold him, and despite the message of his sign, she didn't feel they should hold him. Though he was an enemy, she didn't want him to be a victim of injustice. After all, that was the mission of her group—peace and justice.

"Okay," the detective said, returning with the statement, which he handed to her. "Please read this carefully."

Elsa read the statement, word by word, and found that it was accurate. When she was done she said: "It's fine."

The detective handed her a pen, and she signed the statement.

"Just to bring you up to date, the girl died."

"Oh, Lord have mercy."

"So this is a murder case."

She said a silent prayer for the girl. "Who was she?"

"She was a high school student. Her family was from Haiti. She was black."

"So whoever fired the shot hit her intentionally."

"Yeah, it looks that way." The detective stood on the other side of the table, projecting a controlled feeling of anger.

"What about the guy?"

"We questioned him again, and his story completely agrees with yours. We also have a video from a surveillance camera that shows he didn't fire that shot. And since his eyes were fixed on you, he couldn't have seen who did fire it, so he couldn't *know* who fired it. He could only have an idea who fired it, but he says he doesn't. So we can't hold him."

"Does the video show who did it?"

"No, but we're looking for a video that does. In the meantime this guy will not be allowed to leave the area. I want him available for further questioning."

"Where does he live?"

"His last address was a town in Ohio, but he doesn't live there anymore. It looks like he was traveling with that group."

She had a feeling that the detective hoped she might be able to help him further on the case, and she waited for him to ask her, but all he finally said was: "Thanks for your statement. And give my regards to the sisters at St. Catherine."

"I will." They shook hands, and she followed him out of the interview room.

Outside the precinct Elsa stopped, deliberating what to do. She had done her duty in bearing witness for the guy, and she had no further legal responsibility. Yet she felt a desire to help him in his situation of being far from home and not allowed to leave the area. Where would he stay? Did he have enough money for a hotel?

She was still standing in front of the precinct when he came out. Without the red baseball cap she almost didn't recognize him, but she identified him from his eyes, which stared at her with that look of hatred. For a moment it deterred her, but she broke through it and approached him, saying: "Hi. I'm Elsa."

"I know," he said gruffly. He was several inches taller than her, and he had the body of an athlete. With his blond hair, blue eyes, and white skin he could have been a guy in a television commercial for a sports utility vehicle.

"The detective told you?"

"Yeah, he told me. In fact, he said I should be grateful to you."

"I only did my civic duty. Do you have a place to stay?"

"Why wouldn't I have a place to stay?"

"You're not from here, and you probably didn't plan to stay in the area."

He smiled without humor. "No, I didn't plan to stay in the area. But why should you care what happens to me?"

"I don't need a reason to care about people."

"Oh, I get it. You care about everyone no matter who they are or what they do."

"I wouldn't go that far, but I care enough about you to hope you have a place to stay."

"Well, what if I don't have a place to stay?" he said after a silence, looking as if it had cost him a lot to say this.

"If you don't," she said, "then maybe I could help you."

"How could you help me?"

"I could recommend a place to stay. Hotels in this city are very expensive, but the YMCA is more affordable."

"How much would that cost per night?"

"About a hundred and thirty dollars."

He shook his head. "I don't have enough money for that."

Just then two cops stepped around them on their way into the precinct, prompting Elsa to say: "Let's move away from here."

They walked toward Third Avenue, then stopped and resumed their conversation.

"How much money do you have?" she asked.

He dug into a pocket of his jeans and pulled out a wad of crumpled bills. After counting them he said: "Ninety-two dollars."

"Do you have a credit card?"

"No, I don't. I haven't had a credit card for years."

"Well, where were you planning to stay?"

"At a farm in New Jersey. That's where we met before we came into the city."

"How did you get here?"

"You sound like the detective," he said with a frown.

"I only want to help you go back to that farm."

"I can't go back there."

"Why can't you?"

"They'll kill me."

"Why would they kill you?"

"I talked to the police."

"But you didn't tell them anything."

"I know I didn't," he said, "but they don't know that. They'll think I ratted on the guy who fired that shot."

"Well, the girl died," she said, "so the guy who fired that shot is wanted for murder."

"I know. It's all the more reason why I can't go back there."

She stopped to think. She could use her credit card to pay for the YMCA, but she didn't know how long the police expected him to stay in the area, and she couldn't afford to spend more than a certain amount. She also didn't know if there would even be a room available at the YMCA with all the people visiting the city at this time of year.

She looked at the guy. The look of hatred in his eyes had disappeared, having been replaced by a look of helplessness. This guy was in his early thirties, a grownup man, but right now he seemed like a lost little boy. After making a decision based solely on her instincts, she told him: "Come on."

"Where are we going?"

"We're going to my home."

"Your home?" He looked doubtful. "Where is it?"

"In Yonkers. It's only about fifteen miles from here, so that will satisfy the detective."

Without budging he said: "I couldn't ask you to take me home with you."

"You didn't ask me. I offered to do it."

"But you don't know me."

"I know you well enough," she said with more confidence than she really had. "I know you picked up that gun to prevent anyone else from using it."

His eyes widened. "How do you know that?"

"I just know it. So come on, let's go."

They walked down Third Avenue toward 42nd Street. On the way to Grand Central Station she learned that his name was Karl Reinholdt, and that he was from Freiburg, a town in western Ohio, though he didn't live there anymore. For the past few months he had been traveling with the group that he was with at the demonstration. Its acronym was PWA, which stood for Patriots for a White America.

They didn't talk about their political differences. Instead, they exchanged information about their families. She learned that his family had lived in Ohio for seven generations, and that until his father's generation they had been farmers. He had a younger sister, Angela, a registered nurse who lived in St. Paul, Minnesota. His parents were retired and lived in Boynton Beach, Florida. He didn't mention any other members of his family.

They didn't talk much on the train because there were people around them. When they got to Yonkers, if it had been earlier she would have taken a Bee-Line number six bus, but at this hour it was more convenient to take a taxi. There were several taxis out in front of the Yonkers station, and they got into a gray Crown Victoria, which took them up Broadway to her parent's house. By then she had explained to Karl that she was still living with her parents like so many people of her generation.

While they were on the train she had texted Sister Solana to let her know she was on her way home, she had texted a friend to let her know she was all right, and she had texted her parents to let them know she was bringing a guest. Though it was after ten when the taxi left them off, she knew her parents would still be up. They would have watched the Yankees game, cheering for the Dominicans, and if the game was over, they would be recovering from the excitement, sitting on the sofa and watching the news, her father with a glass of Brugal in his hand.

The front door of the house led into a hallway and then into the living room, where her parents were sitting as she expected.

Her mother jumped up at the sight of her, saying: *"Gracias a Dios! Estábamos tan preocupados por ti."*

"I'm sorry I didn't text you sooner," she said, realizing that her parents must have heard on the news that a girl had been killed at the demonstration.

"Are you all right?"

"Yeah, I'm all right. Karl, this is Yesenia, my mother, and this is Omar, my father. Mom, Dad, this is Karl. I met him at the demonstration. He came all the way from Ohio, and he didn't have a place to stay, so I told him he could stay with us for a few days."

Her father got up from the sofa and respectfully shook Karl's hand, saying: "You came all the way from Ohio? You must be committed to your mission."

Ignoring the blatant irony, Karl only said: "I'm pleased to meet you. And thanks for your hospitality."

"He could sleep in Tirson's room," her mother offered.

"I thought he could have the basement, where he'll have more privacy." The house had a finished basement, with a full bath and a sofa bed. Since the basement was used as a party room, it had a bar and a huge refrigerator that could hold a lot of Presidente beer.

"That's a good idea," her father said.

"Can you tell us about what happened at the demonstration?" her mother asked.

"We didn't see it happen," Elsa said, including Karl and still being truthful. "All we can tell you is that a girl was killed by someone who fired into the crowd."

"They said she was a Haitian, the poor child."

"That's what Sister Solana said. She was a high school student with a group like ours."

"You must be very upset," her father said to Karl. "Would you like a shot of rum?"

"Sure," Karl said as if he was in no position to refuse it.

Elsa sat down in one of the armchairs that flanked the sofa and indicated to Karl that he should take the other.

While her father went to get the rum, her mother asked Karl: "Where in Ohio do you live?"

"I live in a town called Freiburg."

"Does your family live there?"

"My parents used to live there, but now they live in Florida."

"Do you have any brothers or sisters?"

"I have a sister who lives in Minnesota."

"So you're all alone there?"

"Yeah," Karl said with a scratch in his throat. "I have an apartment near where I work."

"Where do you work?"

At this point Karl gave Elsa a look as if he wondered why he was being grilled. She had to smile, knowing what her mother had in mind. Since she had graduated from college, her mother had been pressuring her to get married, and as far as her mother could see, Karl looked like a good candidate.

"Here," her father said, returning with a glass of rum. "It's better than cognac, so I never ruin it with ice or water."

Karl took a sip and nodded to let her father know he liked it.

"Changing the subject," her father said, "Severino won another game."

"He's talking about Luis Severino," she told Karl. "He's the star pitcher for the Yankees. Of course he's Dominican."

"He's from Sábana de la Mar," her father said. "Are you a fan of the Indians or the Reds?"

"The Reds," Karl said. "Our town is closer to Cincinnati than it is to Cleveland."

"The Reds aren't doing very well this year, but the Indians are at the top of their division."

They talked about baseball, a safe subject, until Karl had finished his rum, and then Elsa said: "We're both tired. It's been a stressful day."

"We understand," her mother said. "The sofa bed has clean sheets, so all you have to do is pull it out."

She kissed her mother and her father goodnight, and then she led Karl down to the basement.

"This is nice," he said.

"It's better than the YMCA."

She removed the cushions from the sofa and pulled out the bed. She got a pillow from a closet and made sure there were towels in the bathroom. Then it occurred to her that Karl didn't have clean underwear with him because they were in his backpack at the farm in New Jersey, so she went upstairs and found some briefs and tee shirts in a drawer of the bureau in Tirson's room. She returned with them to the basement and gave them to Karl.

"You know," he said awkwardly, "I really appreciate your kindness."

"You'd do the same for me," she said, believing it.

Her parents were still sitting in their places on the sofa when she returned to the living room. She had a feeling that they had been discussing the guest.

"He seems like a nice young man," her mother said.

"What does he do for a living?" her father asked.

"He works in a factory," she said, lying for the first time. It wasn't a complete lie because she had learned that Karl used to work in a factory before he lost his job two years ago. And she really didn't know what else he did for a living.

"Then he must have some useful skills."

"I'm sure he does. But don't get any ideas," she warned them. "I didn't bring him home as a prospective husband."

"*Que lástima,*" her mother said.

She kissed them goodnight and went upstairs to her bedroom.

After brushing her teeth and putting cream on her skin, she undressed and got into a summer nightgown. She was about to get into bed when she decided to check something. She went to her desk and turned on her laptop, and after it was up and running she did a search on Freiburg, Ohio. The town had a population of 18,342 at the last census. Over the years the population had been declining. According to the demographics section the town was 98.3% white and 1.7% other. There was no mention of Hispanics. In the section on religion she learned that the town was more than two-thirds Catholic, with the rest being mainly Protestants. There was no mention of Jews. And in the section on economics she learned that the town's major employer, a manufacturer of auto body components, had closed its factory two years ago eliminating more than 3,000 jobs, which must have been a fatal blow to the town. She guessed that Karl was one of those people who had lost his job. If so, then that would help to explain his attitude. From her research for her dissertation she had learned about the effects of job loss, especially when it happened suddenly and massively. One of the researchers had used the Kubler-Ross model of grieving to explain what happened to people who lost their jobs from factory closings. According to the model there were five stages: denial, anger, bargaining, depression, and finally acceptance. Since people didn't necessarily go through these stages in a given order, they could be at any stage at any time, so after two years Karl could have moved to the anger stage or been stuck there all along. However he got there, he was clearly at the anger stage.

When you were angry you could direct your anger at anything, including inanimate objects, but you were likely to direct it at the people you blamed for what had happened. It would have been logical to blame the owners of the factory, but anger wasn't logical, and there was a mood in the country now to blame nonwhite immigrants for everything. Given the demographics of Freiburg, it was unlikely that Karl had ever known any nonwhite immigrants, so for him they were only an abstract concept. But then it was probably easier to hate people you had never known than people you had known and lived with.

Shutting down her laptop, she wondered how Karl felt now after being rescued from a night in jail by a brown woman who spoke Spanish as a first language. Did he really appreciate her kindness? Did he see her as a real person? Or was she still only an abstract concept. Unable to resolve this mystery, she slipped into bed and turned off the light on her night table. She lay on her back, staring at the ceiling and remembering their duel of signs. Was there any chance that they could ever understand each other?

She said her usual prayer to Our Lady of Altagracia and then rolled over onto her side. Tomorrow was Sunday, and even though her family lived within two blocks of St. Brigid, they still went to mass at San Pedro, where they had gone when they lived in South Yonkers. They went there out of habit and also because there was a mass in Spanish which her grandmother could understand. This mass was at ten, so tomorrow she would have to tell Karl where they were going and when they would be back. But would he still be there when they got back? Would he steal her mother's jewelry and use the money to go back on the road again?

She was kept awake for a long time by second thoughts about her decision to bring him home.

TWO

LYING ON THE sofa bed, Karl felt drained. He had gotten up at six that morning and attended a chaotic meeting about their plan for the demonstration. There were several groups which didn't agree on many things. In fact, the only thing they all agreed on was the threat to white America from the hordes of nonwhite immigrants invading the country, committing violent crimes, replacing white Americans in jobs, and undermining the values of a great nation. They all supported Donald Trump, who had promised to make America great again, which they understood as making America white again, so they didn't argue about their mission, they argued about tactics and about ridiculous things like who would stand in the front row, who would carry signs, and who would respond to the predictable groups of ultra-liberals that would be there on the other side. On this issue, they agreed not to use violence.

By the time the meeting ended, Karl was already exhausted, though at least he had been assigned to stand in the front row and hold the sign that proclaimed their mission. He wandered away from the parking area where they had held the meeting and went into the dilapidated barn, where he hoped to be alone. He was sitting on a bale of hay when his peace was disrupted by the entrance into the barn of Junior Ritchie, a nutcase from West Virginia who was a member of the Ku Klux Klan. He was a scrawny man in his mid-fifties with a low forehead and a slack jaw, but there was fire in his glaucous eyes.

"What did you think of the meeting?" he asked after settling next to Karl on the bale.

"I didn't like it," Karl said. "I don't like meetings."

"Well, I didn't like the way we chickened out at the end."

"What do you mean?"

"I mean agreeing not to use violence."

"We'll be in New York City, where they have cops all over the place. We couldn't get away with anything there."

"Maybe you couldn't, but I could." He pulled out a gun from a deep pocket in his carpenter's pants. It was a German luger, which he fondled as if he was playing with himself. "You see this? It's not registered to anyone, so it can't be traced."

"But if you used it, they'd grab you in a second."

"No, they wouldn't. I'd get rid of it, so they wouldn't catch me with it."

Karl was skeptical. "How would you use it?"

"I'd shoot me a nigger."

Never having known a black, Karl didn't feel the personal animosity against them that his companions from the South displayed. He hated blacks as a matter of principle, but he had never felt like killing one of them. And he wondered if Junior was serious. "Why would you want to kill a black?"

"To get rid of one. The more niggers we get rid of, the whiter we'll make our country."

"But there are forty million of them in our country. You can't kill all of them."

"I can't by myself," Junior said, "but if pussies like you joined me, we could get that number down, and then we could send the rest of them back to Africa."

"Well, if I were you," Karl told him, "I wouldn't use that gun in New York."

"You're not me, thank the good Lord."

Remembering this conversation and recognizing the gun that had landed on the street in front of him, Karl was sure that Junior was the one who fired the shot that killed the black girl. But he said nothing about it to the detective. He simply insisted that he hadn't seen who fired the shot, and that was the truth.

He had reasons for not telling the detective about Junior, as despicable as the man was. One reason was his loyalty to the movement. As a member of the union at the factory he had never betrayed a fellow member, no matter what. For him, betrayal was a major sin. Another reason was his reluctance to get involved with a murder case. With all his other problems, getting involved in a murder case was the last thing he needed, and he understood the law well enough to know that being a witness could get you into trouble. The final reason was his fear of what would happen to him if he told the police about Junior. He had already decided not to go back to the farm because of what they might do to him, even though he could swear to them that he hadn't ratted on a member of their group.

His big mistake was picking up the gun. He had acted on an impulse to prevent anyone else from using the gun because he knew that some of the other guys were as crazy as Junior in their own ways, but it had been a stupid thing to do. He should have known that being caught with the gun in his hand would make him the prime suspect. If he hadn't picked up that goddam gun, he wouldn't be in his present situation, dependent on the kindness of nonwhite immigrants who he believed should never have been permitted to enter the country. If he hadn't acted on that impulse, he wouldn't have to remain in the area until the detective allowed him to leave. He would be free to pursue his mission of making America white again.

And how long would he be in this situation? How many nights would he have to spend with this Dominican family before the detective allowed him to leave?

He was awakened the next morning by Elsa, who discreetly called to him from the stairway, saying: "It's nine thirty, and we're going to mass. There's a clean towel for you to take a shower, and there's food in the kitchen for your breakfast. It's mango season, so I hope you like mangos. The bread's fresh. The coffee's Dominican."

"Okay," he muttered. "Thanks."

"We should be back by eleven thirty."

"Okay. I'll see you then."

He waited until she disappeared before getting out of bed. He felt as if he had a hangover, and he was encouraged by the thought of coffee. But Dominican coffee? He had thought all coffee came from Colombia and Brazil.

As he stood in the shower he thought about this family going to mass. Like most people in Freiburg, he had been raised as a Catholic, but the last time he had gone to church was for his daughter's first communion, a year before the factory closed. Among other reasons for not going to church, he blamed God for letting his whole life be ruined. He felt a mixture of scorn and envy for these people who evidently still believed that God was love.

He put on the underwear that Elsa had brought him, then his shirt and his jeans. He took his cell phone out of the left pocket of his jeans and turned it on. The charger was in his backpack at the farm, so he had to ration his use of the phone. There were no messages, so he turned off the phone. The police had taken it and presumably downloaded his contacts, which they would be checking. They wouldn't find Junior among his contacts since he and Junior had never exchanged messages. In any case, since the gun wasn't registered to Junior, the police wouldn't suspect him more than anyone else in the group, except for his being a Klan member. Karl had never met a Klan member before, though they said you could find them in southern Ohio.

He went upstairs and into the kitchen, where he found a bowl of cutup yellow fruit on the table and a plate with slices of Italian bread. A percolator was on the stove, so presumably all he had to do was turn on the burner under it to make coffee. A bag of coffee was on the counter with its brand name in red letters on a white background: Santo Domingo. He opened the bag and smelled the coffee. It promised to be good, but often coffee didn't taste as good as it smelled.

He turned on the burner under the percolator and sat down at the table and helped himself to some yellow fruit. He had never tasted mango before, and he really liked it. Assuming that it was all for him, he finished the bowl and reached for the bread. There was butter and jam for it. With only butter on it, he ate a slice of bread. He hadn't eaten since yesterday morning, and the bread helped to abate his hunger. By then the coffee was ready, and he poured it into a white mug that they had left on the table for him. There was writing on the side of the mug which said: *"Amarás a tu prójimo como a ti mismo."* He didn't understand what it meant, but he guessed it had to do with love.

While he sipped the coffee, which was just as good as it had smelled, he tried to reconcile his image of nonwhite immigrants with the reality of Elsa and her parents. The difference seemed much too great for the truth to lie between the two extremes, so either his image of nonwhite immigrants was wrong or Elsa and her parents were faking it.

But why would they fake it? To refute his patriotic arguments against allowing nonwhite immigrants in this country? To prove that his image of them was wrong? This explanation might be far-fetched, but Elsa knew what his mission was, and she had opposed it there on the street by lifting her sign in response to his sign, so maybe they were only being kind to him to show that nonwhite immigrants were good people.

Hoping to escape from his torturous thoughts, he reached for the newspaper that was lying on the table. The headline of the lead story said: "Girl Killed at Rally." According to the story, some faith-based groups were peacefully protesting against the government's immigration policies when some far-right groups arrived to oppose them. A shot was fired, killing a high school girl whose parents were immigrants from Haiti. The police were asking people who might have observed the shot being fired to come forward and provide information.

That let Karl off the hook, at least in a technical sense. He hadn't observed the shot being fired, so he didn't really *know* who had done it. But he was beginning to question his reasons for not telling the police what he did know.

He was still at the table when he heard the front door open.

It was Elsa, her parents, and her grandmother returning from church. She led the way into the kitchen.

"Did you find everything you needed?" she asked him.

"Oh, yeah. The coffee was good, and I liked the mango. I never tasted one before."

"Then you've been leading a deprived life."

"I guess I have," he said, managing to smile in response to her teasing.

"This is Bela, my grandmother," she said, putting an arm around an older woman who came into the kitchen after her.

"I'm pleased to meet you," Karl said, rising from his chair.

"Don't get up for me," the woman said with a heavy accent. To her granddaughter she said: *"Es muy guapo. Es tu novio?"*

"No es mi novio. Es solo un amigo."

"Qué lástima."

"We're having our usual Sunday dinner," Elsa told him. "My brother won't be here because he's spending the weekend with friends."

"Since you only got here last night," Yesenia said, "I didn't have time to make *sancocho*, but we'll have chicken with rice and beans. You like chicken?"

"Yeah, anything's fine."

"We usually eat around one, so you have time to relax for a while."

"Come and join us on the deck," Omar told him. "We need to get out of the cook's way."

Karl got up and followed Elsa and Omar out to the deck, which overlooked a lawn that had a boundary of fir trees around it. There were several chairs with seats and backs of plastic strips, and after Omar had taken one of them, Karl took another.

"Did you sleep well?" Omar asked him.

"Yeah, I did. I was exhausted."

"Demonstrations take a lot of energy," Elsa said, apparently without any irony.

"You're welcome to stay here until you're ready for the trip home," Omar said. "Will you travel by plane?"

"No, I'll get a ride from someone."

"Elsa said you work in a factory. What do you make there?"

"We make components for auto bodies."

"Where do you send them?"

"To assembly factories in this country and in Mexico."

"It's too bad they don't assemble cars in the Dominican Republic. It would be good for the economy."

"They don't have a big enough market there," Elsa said as if she knew something about economics.

"Then maybe they could assemble *motos*. They should have a big enough market for them."

"He's talking about motorbikes."

"I guessed that," Karl said.

"But they make some good products," Omar said. "The coffee, the cigars, the rum, and the beer are the best in the world."

"Don't forget the baseball players," Elsa said.

"Yeah, they're by far the best in the world. Speaking of which, the Yankees are playing this afternoon."

"You're not allowed to listen to the game during dinner."

"Yeah, I know. But I can catch the last few innings."

"Would you like a beer?" Elsa asked him.

"I don't know. I guess if other people are having one."

"I'm having one, and Dad's having one. We always drink beer with our Sunday dinner."

"Presidente," Omar said. "The best beer in the whole world."

The dinner was excellent. The chicken was roasted perfectly, and the rice and beans were a new experience. They were so much better than the yellow rice and refried beans that Karl had eaten in Mexican restaurants.

He also noticed that the family, including the grandmother, kept talking with each other during the whole meal, often more than one of them at the same time. There were only four of them, but it sounded like there were ten of them. It was so different from the mostly silent dinners Karl remembered from his own family.

After dinner, while Elsa helped her mother in the kitchen, Karl joined her father on the deck, where he was offered a cigar and a glass of rum. He declined the cigar but accepted the rum. And they sat down with the radio tuned to the Yankees game, which was at the bottom of the sixth inning, with the Yankees up.

They listened until the game was over. By then Karl had

finished his rum and was feeling sleepy, so he asked: "Is it okay if I lie down for a while?"

"No problem," Omar said. "It's time for a siesta."

Karl went down to the basement, kicked off his shoes, and lay down on the sofa bed. He didn't want to sleep, he only wanted to gather his thoughts and deal with his situation. But instead of focusing on the present, his mind wandered back to the past, to the event that had changed his life.

The company had been owned by the same family for six generations. It had started by making parts for horse-drawn carriages, and over the years it had evolved into a manufacturer of components for auto bodies. While Karl was growing up the company was by far the largest employer in the town. Its three thousand workers directly supported as many families, who accounted for almost half of the town's population, and in turn their spending supported all of the town's businesses, including supermarkets, pharmacies, restaurants, bars, and clothing stores. Above all, the company was the town's major taxpayer, supporting all of the government services, including the police, the fire department, the schools, and the library. So without the company the town of Freiburg couldn't survive.

Luckily for the town, the owners of the company were responsible, effective managers, and their business prospered, weathering the world wars, the Depression, and the disruptions of the auto industry. It probably would have weathered the Great Recession that began in 2008 if it hadn't been weakened by a falling out among the owners, which began with the untimely death of the owner-manager who steered the company through the recession that began in the year after Karl started working for the company. There was no clear succession plan, so there was a power struggle among the five heirs that left the company without a leader for several years. The heirs finally resolved their conflict by selling the company to a private equity group, and within a year they all left town with their share of the money, no doubt anticipating how they would be regarded by the town they had abandoned.

Two years later, Karl's parents accepted buyouts from the new owners, who were cutting costs in order to position the company for a resale. His father, who had worked at the company for forty years, received a full pension and one month's pay for every year he had worked there, and his mother, who had worked there for thirty-one years, received the same benefits, so they got out at the right time in view of what happened later. Within six months his parents sold their house and moved to Boynton Beach, where they could live comfortably and not have to deal with Ohio winters. At the time Karl had been working at the company for twelve years, was married, and had two young children, so he could only hope that the new owners would be able to turn the company around.

They did manage to make the company profitable again, and as soon as they did, they sold the company to another private equity group. This sale, like the previous sale, was financed by debt incurred by the company, so now it was very highly leveraged, a concept that Karl learned the hard way. The debt was in the form of bonds that were held by people who specialized in high-risk securities and who evidently bought the bonds with the hope of acquiring the assets of the company through a default. Inevitably, though the company had earnings before interest payments, the time came when it was unable to pay the interest on its debt, and the bondholders initiated the process of bankruptcy.

"What will happen?" Karl asked the union steward during a lunch break. They were eating in the company cafeteria.

"They'll close the factory," the steward said, "and they'll sell the equipment to Mexico."

"You mean they'll make the components in Mexico?"

"The bondholders won't, but someone will."

"Well, what about the buildings?"

"They'll try to sell them to a developer."

"But if they close the factory," Karl said, "there won't be any development in this town."

"Yeah, I know. But they'll recover what they paid for the bonds from our cash, our accounts receivable, our inventory, and what they get from selling our furniture and equipment. So they can sit on the buildings forever."

Wondering how his parents might be affected, Karl asked: "What about the pensions?"

"They're not fully funded, so people on pensions won't get the full amount. There's federal insurance, but it won't cover all of their losses."

"Why aren't the pensions fully funded?"

"Because the money was used for other things."

Karl was outraged. "Is that legal?"

"Yeah, it's legal, unless there was fraud. In any case, it's not right. But a lot of companies have underfunded pensions. In fact, a lot of states have them."

"It's not right. You work all your life and count on a pension and then they take it away from you because the money was used for other things? For me, that's a crime."

"This whole thing is a crime," the steward said. "The original owners walked away with millions of dollars that the company borrowed, and the next owners walked away with millions of dollars that the company borrowed, and now these owners will walk away with millions of dollars from the company's assets. For me, that's pillage and looting."

"And there's nothing we can do about it?"

"There's nothing we can do about it. That's how the capitalist system works."

It didn't take the bondholders long to close the factory. By then there were fewer employees, but according to the union steward, two thousand eight hundred and seventeen people lost their jobs, including Karl and the coworkers who were his friends, and his parents lost about half of their pensions.

The town was devastated. The clothing stores closed, the pharmacies closed, the restaurants closed, almost everything closed except for the bars. The police and the firemen had to take a pay cut. The schools had trouble paying the teachers. The number of garbage collections was reduced. The predominant feeling in the town was anger, which found an outlet in a raging fire that burned down the unoccupied mansion of the family that had owned the company.

A lot of people left the town to find jobs elsewhere, but a hard core of people remained, and Karl was among them. Initially, his refusal to leave was based on his feeling that because his family had lived in the county for seven generations, he had a right to live there. And then it evolved into a feeling that he had a right to have a job there, and not just any old job but the job he had been doing when the factory closed. So his anger began to focus on the people who had made him lose his job. The first targets of his anger were the bondholders who had put the company out of business. There was no way of knowing who they were, so he directed his feeling against all bondholders. Then there were the private equity groups that had used the company to borrow money and pay themselves millions. But there was no way of knowing who they were, so he simply hated capitalists.

This feeling got him into an argument in a bar where he went too often now. He was drinking beer with a former co-worker and railing about capitalists when a guy at the end of the bar said: "You don't know what you're talking about."

"What do you mean?" he asked defensively.

"The problem isn't capitalists. The founders of our company were capitalists, and without them we wouldn't have had a company. We wouldn't have had jobs."

"Then what's the problem?"

"The problem is our financial system which allows people to do what they did to our company."

"You mean have our company borrow money so that they could take it?"

"Right. If they hadn't been allowed to do that, we'd still have a company. We'd still have our jobs."

"But how were they allowed to do that?"

"Our financial system allowed them to do that. It allowed them to get rich at our expense."

"Who created our financial system?"

"Politicians created it. They were paid by people like the ones who fucked us."

"Are you saying that politicians were *paid* to create a system that could be used to fuck us?

"Of course they were. Where have you been?"

He paused to absorb this revelation. "So we should blame the politicians."

"Yeah, we should blame the politicians. I mean, both parties. They're both playing the same game."

"And what's the game."

"To stay in power indefinitely and amass wealth at the expense of working people."

"Okay," Karl said. "So what can we do about the politicians?"

"We can throw them out of office and replace them with a party that cares about working people."

"Would it be a new party?"

"Yeah, it would be a revolutionary party."

"You don't mean communist."

The guy laughed harshly. "No, that's old hat. I mean a party led by someone from outside the system."

"Do you have someone in mind?"

"No. But someone will emerge. Just wait and see."

Lying there on the sofa bed, Karl remembered what the guy had said, and now it seemed prophetic. Someone had emerged from outside the system, and he had formed a government that cared about working people. He was doing things for working people like protecting them from the damage caused by foreign trade and immigration. If things kept going in the right direction, then we wouldn't import auto body components from Mexico, we would make them in our own country, at the factory in Freiburg, and he would get his job back.

Before getting up, he reached for his cell phone, which he had set on the bedside table. Propped on his elbow, he turned on the phone and saw that there was a new message. It was from a sender that he didn't recognize, but as soon as he read the message he knew who had sent it. The message said: "You're a dead man, and so is anyone who helps you."

Of course it was Junior, who evidently had gotten his phone number from the list of contacts for their group, and he could be at the farm now, or he could be anywhere.

Karl immediately turned off his phone, having heard that you could be tracked if your phone was on and not knowing if Junior might have that capability. He doubted that Junior had it, but he couldn't be sure.

For some reason he was concerned most by the second part of the message, which was a threat against Elsa and her family, and he decided without a second thought that he couldn't put them at risk by his presence here.

He rolled off the bed and went upstairs, where he found Elsa and her parents in the living room, sitting and talking with their usual animation.

"Did you have a good rest?" her father asked him.

"Yeah, I did. Could I see you for a minute?" he said to Elsa.

"Sure," she said, getting up from her chair.

They went out to the deck, where they were out of the hearing range of her parents.

"I can't stay here," he told her.

"You can't? Why not?"

"Well, I just got a text message from the guy who killed that Haitian girl."

With a frown she said: "I thought you didn't know who did it."

"I didn't see him do it, but I know he did it. It was his gun that landed on the pavement in front of me. And before we left the farm, he said he was going to kill a nigger."

"You didn't tell the police about this."

"No, I didn't. I know I should have, but— It's hard to explain. At the time I felt it was right not to tell them."

"Do you still feel that way?"

"I don't know. I have to think about it. But the thing is, he threatened to kill me, and he also threatened to kill anyone who helps me."

From her face he could tell she gulped on that. "He did?"

"Yeah. I don't think he knows where I am, but he could find out, and I don't want to put you and your family at risk."

"I understand. But where would you go?"

"I'd go somewhere out of the area."

She shook her head firmly. "That wouldn't solve the problem. And it would get you into trouble with the police."

"It would solve the problem of this guy's threat to you and your family."

"It might not. I mean, even if you went away, if he found out that you were here, he could still harm us. So the only way to solve the problem is for the police to catch this guy. And if you can help them catch him, you should do it."

"Maybe I should, but right now I have to get out of here."

"Okay." She paused. "If I find a place to hide you, then you won't have to leave the area."

"Well, find it soon. We don't have much time."

She furrowed her brow, and after a while her eyes brightened. "I have an idea."

"What is it?" he asked.

"Give me a minute. I have to talk with Sister Solana." She took her phone out of the pocket of her jeans and punched in a number.

From her face he could tell that the phone was ringing at the other end.

"Sister? It's Elsa. *Necesito un favor…*Yeah, it does…I'll explain when I see you. *La casa de huéspedes está disponible?…* It is? *Gracias a Dios…*I'll be there in about fifteen minutes." Looking relieved, she shut off her phone.

"Can you tell me what you have in mind?"

"I'll tell you when we get there." She went into the kitchen and got a plastic bag and told him: "Go down to the basement and put your things into this bag."

While he was in the basement doing this she must have talked to her parents because when he returned to the living room they were on their feet.

"Elsa told us something came up and you have to go," her mother said with a look of concern. "We hope it's not serious."

"No, it's not serious. But it *is* urgent."

"Well, we enjoyed meeting you, and we hope to see you again sometime."

"I hope to see you again too. And thanks for your hospitality. You saved my life."

Of course they didn't think he meant that literally.

Her mother kissed him on the cheek, and her father shook his hand, and then they went out to Elsa's car, a blue Honda Civic.

As she backed the car out of the driveway with him in the passenger seat, he knew his life was in her hands, and amazingly, he trusted her.

THREE

THE COLLEGE CAMPUS was only a five-minute drive from Elsa's house, immediately north of the hospital where the nursing students did their clinical work. The campus was on a hundred acres of land at the bluff that overlooked the Hudson River. The land and several buildings were bequeathed to the college by the Morrissey family, which had made their fortune in trade and finance during the nineteenth century. Their mansion, which was made with local gray stone, was now the administrative building of the college. Their garage, made with the same stone, was the office of facilities management. The house and garage were now accompanied by classroom buildings, dormitories, a field house, a student center, and a convent, all of them in matching red brick, with plenty of land left over for athletic fields and parking.

The college was founded by the Sisters of the Redemption shortly after the second world war with donations from Catholic families, led by the Morrisseys. Originally, it was for women only, but in the early seventies it went co-ed, along with many other colleges that had been single sex. It had about seven thousand students now, with schools of education, business, the health professions, social and behavioral sciences, and the liberal arts. It was still Catholic, but for the first time it didn't have a sister as president, it had a lay person, a male Latino who was a graduate of the college.

"This is where I work," Elsa told Karl as they entered the campus. She waved to the security guard who recognized her car so he didn't have to check it for a sticker. With all the school shootings, the college had tightened its security over the past few years.

"What kind of work do you do?" Karl asked her.

"I teach, and I counsel students."

"What do you teach?"

"Psychology."

"And what do you counsel students about?"

"About their problems. They're kids," she added, "and they're growing up in a scary world."

"What kind of problems do they have?"

"All kinds of problems. For one thing, more than half of them are from families below the poverty level. So they have financial problems."

"Then how can they afford college?"

"They get grants from the federal government and the state, and they get scholarships from the college for whatever is left. So they can attend college free."

"How can you afford to do that?"

"We work hard, we control expenses, and we get donations from people who still believe in the kind of education we offer."

She pulled into a parking spot that was near the convent. At this time of year there were plenty of parking spots available because the dormitories were closed for the summer and only a small number of courses were running. In the fall and spring semesters you needed a strategy to find a parking spot.

Sister Solana was waiting for her in front of the convent, standing near a statue of the Blessed Mother. The sister's family was from the Dominican Republic, like Elsa's family and like the families of many undergraduate students. Though she was in the school of business, she also taught courses in religion, ethics, and psychology. She had been Elsa's mentor, not only for academic matters but also for life matters. In fact, the sister had helped her through a difficult period that at times of crisis still reverberated in her mind.

"Hi," Sister Solana said with her radiant smile. The nuns no longer wore habits, so the only indication that Sister Solana might be a nun was the plain wooden cross that hung from a lanyard around her neck outside her shirt. The cross had been carved from an ancient olive tree in the town of Bethlehem.

"Sister Solana, this is Karl Reinholdt," she said, introducing him.

"I'm pleased to meet you," the sister said, shaking his hand.

"I think I saw you at the demonstration," Karl told her.

"Yeah, I was there. And I saw you."

There was an awkward silence, then Elsa said: "The police told Karl not to leave the area, and he didn't have any place to stay, so I brought him home with me last night. But today he got a message from the guy who killed that Haitian girl. It was a threat to kill him and anyone who helps him."

"Lord have mercy," the sister said.

"So we have to hide him until the police catch that guy."

"Well, as I told you, the guesthouse is available. We don't have any scheduled guests until the end of the summer."

"We use the guesthouse," Elsa explained, "for visitors from out of town. It saves money on hotel rooms."

"I have the key," the sister said, "so I can let you in. You don't have a backpack?"

"He left it at the farm where his group assembled."

"Then he'll need clothes."

"I gave him briefs and tee shirts from my brother, but if he's going to stay for a while, he'll need more things."

"I hope I don't have to stay long," Karl told them. "I mean, you're very nice, but I can't just sit here doing nothing."

"We'll talk about that later," the sister said, leading the way.

The guesthouse was made with the same stone as the house and the garage. It had been the caretaker's house when the Morrissey family had lived there. It had two bedrooms, a full bath, a kitchen, and a living room. It was equipped with a flat-screen television and a laptop computer connected to the internet.

"This is nice," Karl said when he saw it.

"It's nicer than our basement," Elsa admitted.

"There are clean sheets and clean towels," Sister Solana said. "There's soap and shampoo and even a toothbrush like you get at hotels."

They followed the sister on a tour of the house, and as the two women lingered in the bathroom Elsa said: "Thanks for helping me. I didn't know what else to do."

"*No hay problema.* I think it's a good use for the guesthouse. He's a visitor from out of town, and he's a representative from the other side, so maybe he can help us understand them."

"Yeah, maybe he can."

Back in the living room the sister said to Karl: "For our records, I need the name of your organization."

"Patriots for a White America," he said proudly.

"I'll give you credit for having the honesty to say that to a nonwhite woman, but after you're settled I'd like to hear more about these patriots."

"That's fine. Just so you know, I was raised as a Catholic, so you don't have to convert me."

"Don't worry. That's not my intention."

Elsa followed the sister outside, where they could talk without being heard. "We're doing the right thing, aren't we?"

"I think we are. Remember what Jesus said about loving our enemies."

"I don't love him, I only feel bad for him. I mean, I feel something must have happened to him that made him get involved with those people."

"What do you know about him?"

"I know he's from Freiburg, Ohio, where he had a job in a factory. I know that a big factory in that town closed about two years ago, and I think that's how he lost his job. But I can't make any connection between losing his job and hating immigrants."

"He didn't lose his job to immigrants?"

"No. That town is almost a hundred percent white, so I don't see how he could have even met an immigrant."

"Mm. Well, maybe there's something else that he blames on immigrants."

"Yeah, maybe. You know," she said after thinking for a moment, "it must be very hard for him to accept what we're doing for him."

"It must be," Sister Solana agreed. "But he *is* accepting it, at least so far. And that could lead to a reconciliation."

"That's what I want. I don't want to convert him to our side. I just want him to realize that immigrants are human beings."

"Unless his ancestors were Native Americans, they must have been immigrants."

"He didn't say anything about his ancestors. He only said that his family had lived in Ohio for seven generations."

"That's a long time. But his family must have come from another country, so while he's staying in our guesthouse with nothing else to do, we should encourage him to use that computer and do some research on his ancestors."

"You mean if he can connect with them, then maybe he can connect with us?"

"That's the idea. It's all about making connections."

She hugged the sister, thanked her, and went back into the guesthouse, where she found Karl slouched on the sofa gazing at the blank television screen.

"How are you doing?" she asked him.

"I'm doing okay," he said glumly.

"You need some clothes. If you stand up, I can see if you're close to my brother's size."

"I don't want to take your brother's clothes."

"Just stand up and be quiet," she said as if he was one of her students.

He finally stood up, though his shoulders were slumped.

Judging from the location of his head in relation to hers, she figured he was about the same height as Tirson, and he was only a little stockier. With luck, her brother's shirts and pants would fit him, though looking ahead, she saw the need to buy him clothes that he could take with him after the killer was in custody.

Next, she addressed the issue of food. The guesthouse had a refrigerator, a stove, and a toaster oven, but there was no food in the cupboards.

"What do you eat?" she asked Karl.

He shrugged. "I don't know. Whatever I can get."

"Do you know how to cook?"

"I can fry eggs."

"I don't know how long you'll be here, but we need to buy some groceries for you." She found a notepad near the telephone, along with a pen. "Let's make a list. We can start with eggs. What kind of bread do you like?"

"Any kind."

"You must have a preference."

"I like normal bread."

"You mean white bread?"

They exchanged a look. "That's normal bread isn't it?"

"It's normal for people who like it white, but there are other kinds of bread."

"I got the message."

"White bread," she said, writing it down. "If I get tuna and mayonnaise, then you could use the bread to make tuna salad sandwiches."

He started to say something but abruptly stopped. "Yeah. I could make tuna salad sandwiches."

"When you're with your group, what do you eat?"

"We mainly eat fast food."

"Well, you can't eat fast food here."

"When we cook we usually have hotdogs or hamburgers."

"I'll get hotdogs. They're easier. Do you like pasta?"

"I like spaghetti and meat balls."

"Do you know how to cook spaghetti?"

"I've cooked it," he said, for some reason not looking at her. There was evidently something he wasn't telling her.

"What do you drink?"

"I drink beer."

"What kind of beer?"

"Bud Light."

"Is that what you usually drink?"

"It's what I always drink."

"Well, there are other kinds of beer," she said, smiling, "but if you want Bud Light, I'll get it for you. Cans or bottles?"

"I prefer cans. They don't take up so much room in the fridge."

"Okay." She wrote: "Bud Light - cans."

To the list she added toilet paper, which she had noticed was running low, and paper towels and dishwashing liquid.

When the list was finally completed she left Karl in the guesthouse and drove to the local supermarket, which was only a few blocks from the college. It was owned by her father and her uncle. It was one of the four supermarkets they operated in Yonkers, not counting the bodega where they had started their business. It was only a midsized supermarket, but it had everything you needed. And it had good prices, especially with the family discount.

As Elsa filled her shopping cart with items from the list she recalled how Karl had acted during their recent conversation. She could easily imagine how guys on the road, travelling from one demonstration to the next, would live on fast food, but in his replies to her questions about tuna and spaghetti he seemed to avoid revealing anything about his life before he joined the movement. He was in his early thirties, he must have worked at that factory for a while, and he probably wasn't living alone all that time. There must have been a woman, a girlfriend or a wife, who cooked for him. Since he hadn't mentioned her, then he must have been hurt by whatever had happened. She knew from her own experience what it was like to be hurt from a relationship, so she could empathize with him.

She bought some things that weren't on the list, including orange juice and bananas. He had liked the coffee at her house, so she bought Santo Domingo for him, and though she bought a six-pack of Bud Light cans, she also got a six-pack of Presidente in green bottles. In her unbiased opinion, there was no comparison between the two beers.

When she returned with the groceries she found Karl sitting on the sofa, watching Fox News. A man with a look of hatred in his eyes was ranting about the liberal elites who had ruined the country. He sounded like the braying burro she had heard on a visit to the *campo* where her grandmother had grown up.

Whether or not he sensed her reaction, Karl turned off the television remotely and got up to join her in the kitchen, where she was unloading the groceries.

"What's this?" he asked, lifting a green bottle halfway from its six-pack.

"It's Presidente, the beer we were drinking at my house."

"I thought you were getting Bud Light."

"I got it, but I also got Presidente." She offered him the rolls of toilet paper. "Put these in the bathroom. Okay?"

"Okay," he said, taking them from her.

When they had put everything away, she had an idea. "If you get bored watching Fox News, you could use the computer."

"I don't know how to use a computer."

"You don't?" She was surprised. "How come?"

He shrugged. "I never had any use for it."

"Well, I'll show you how to use it." She led him to the desk, pulled up a chair alongside of the chair at the desk, and sat down with him. "Now, this is how you turn it on."

They waited for the computer to go through the process of booting up.

"You see this? It's an icon for a browser. I recommend using this one," she said, clicking on it. "Now, if you want to search for something, you just enter it into this line. Tell me what you'd like to search for."

"How about beer?"

"Okay." She typed in the word and tapped the enter button. The top entry was Wikipedia.

"What's Wikipedia?"

"It's an online encyclopedia. If you want to read it, you click on it." She clicked on it, and the text began: "Beer is one of the oldest and most widely consumed alcoholic drinks in the world, and the third most popular drink overall after water and tea."

"I can see why water would be ahead of beer, but why tea?"

"They drink it in China and India."

"Oh, yeah. They have billions of people. They work for less than a dollar an hour."

Avoiding that particular issue, she said: "So you can do research on anything you want. Like immigration."

"Why would I want to do research on that?"

"To learn about your ancestors. Now, when you're done using the computer, you don't turn it off, you shut it down." She showed him how.

"Well, thanks," he said. "I can tell you're a teacher."

By now it was after six, and her parents would be wondering what happened to her. Though at her age she chafed at having to keep her parents informed on her whereabouts, at the same time she appreciated the security of living at home with a family who cared about her. She texted her mother to let her know she was on her way home, and before leaving she made sure that Karl had everything he needed.

"What if I need to contact you?" he asked. "I can't use my cell phone."

"Use the landline here. Just dial nine to call outside."

"I probably won't need to contact you, but you never know."

"You never know," she agreed. She gave him her cell phone number, and she entered the extension of the guesthouse phone into her electronic phonebook.

There was an awkward moment when if she had been with a friend, she would have kissed the person on the cheek and said goodbye, but this guy wasn't a friend, though she no longer regarded him as an enemy. He was somewhere in between, and maybe he was moving in the right direction.

She got home in time to join her parents and her grandmother for the light supper they had on Sundays. For their own protection she let her parents assume that she had dropped Karl off at the train station—it was better for them not to know where he was. And she fended off their favorable comments about him.

Before they got up from the table her mother reminded her that Bela had an appointment with the eye doctor at nine the next morning. Her mother couldn't take her because she had a meeting with the firm that provided accounting services for the family business. Her mother was very good with numbers and very good with money. From her mother Elsa had learned that in their home country women often handled the money for a family business, presumably because they could be trusted with money more than men.

While she was getting ready for bed, Elsa thought about Karl and wondered if he was all right. She was tempted to call him and check on him, but she resisted the impulse, reminding herself that he wasn't a child. And she didn't want to give him the wrong impression. Instead, she called Sister Solana and asked her to check on him in the morning, explaining that she had to take her grandmother to the eye doctor. Sister Solana responded positively, as if she welcomed the opportunity to talk with this man from the other side.

Before going to sleep she heard her brother come home from his weekend at Montauk. She was too tired to talk with him, so she didn't call to him and ask about his weekend. He had a lot of friends, with a progression of girlfriends who lasted until they got serious about him. Right now he didn't have a girlfriend.

The next morning after breakfast she drove her grandmother to the eye clinic, which was about twenty minutes away. A month ago the eye doctor had removed a cataract from Bela's left eye and replaced the lens. The procedure had gone well, and this was a follow-up appointment to make sure that everything was all right.

As they drove north on the Saw Mill Parkway her grandmother said. "*Es un milagro.* I have perfect vision in this eye."

"It *is* a miracle," Elsa agreed. "A miracle of science."

"It wasn't science. It was the Lord's will for me to see again with this eye."

"So it was both science and the Lord's will. But since the Lord isn't with us now to perform a miracle and restore your sight, it helped to have science."

"The Lord is always with us. And all science is from the Lord, as the pope says. It's the Lord's way of helping us."

"If the pope said that, I can accept it."

"You should read what he says."

"I've read some of it, but I guess I should read more of it."

Elsa was a serious Catholic, and beyond going to mass every Sunday she helped Sister Solana with the community services at

San Pedro and with the political activities of Students for Peace and Justice, for which she recruited members to participate in demonstrations. But she still felt inadequate compared with her grandmother.

Prompted by this feeling, she made a decision. "If I tell you something, will you promise not to tell Mom and Dad?"

"We shouldn't have secrets," Bela said uncomfortably.

"I only want to tell you because I think you'll understand."

"You don't think your parents would understand?"

"I think they would, but I don't want to worry them."

"You don't mind worrying me?"

"It's not that," Elsa said, "it's just that I think you can take it."

"I'm sure they could take it. You have no idea how tough they are."

She remembered how they had supported her after her meltdown, and she had to admit that Bela was right. But in that situation she had told Bela about it first. Both then and now she felt that her grandmother, being a generation removed from her, could deal with her situations without feeling directly responsible as her parents did.

"Is it about that guy?" Bela asked as they were waiting for a traffic light to change. It was one of the longer lights on the parkway because for some reason a developer had built a major project there with apartment buildings, stores, a restaurant, and a movie theater.

"It's about him, but it's not what you think."

"How do you know what I think?"

"I don't know, but after what happened to me—"

"I don't remember what happened to you. Whatever it was, it's long forgotten."

"Okay." She inhaled deeply and exhaled. "It was true when I told my parents I met that guy at the demonstration, but he's not on our side. He's on the other side."

"I'm not surprised."

"Why aren't you surprised?"

"Well, for one thing, he's white."

"We have white people on our side."

"I know. But they're educated white people. That guy doesn't seem educated."

"He doesn't," she agreed. "He probably didn't go beyond high school."

"It's not how far he went in school. I didn't go beyond fifth grade, and the school was only a one-room shack. But at least I know a few things about the world."

"What do you know that he doesn't know?"

"I know that the world has changed."

At that moment the light turned green and she lifted her foot off the brake.

"As you know," she continued with the car moving forward, "a girl was killed at that demonstration. That guy didn't do it, but the police thought he did, and they took him into custody. I knew he hadn't done it because I was standing across the street from him, and I didn't take my eyes off him for even a second. So I went to the precinct and got him released."

"You did what Jesus said we should do—love our enemies."

"I don't love him, but I believe in justice, and I didn't want him to be accused unjustly of killing that girl."

"You did the right thing," Bela told her. "I'm glad you told me, and I won't tell your parents. But I assume you'll tell them sooner or later."

"I will. I just don't want them to worry now."

"What would they worry about?"

She hesitated, then said: "They'd worry about what might happen to me for helping that guy."

"You mean the police might think you were involved?"

"No. The guys he was with might think he told the police who killed that girl."

"So they'd want to harm him?"

"Yeah, they'd want to harm him. And they'd want to harm anyone who helps him."

"But you took him to the train station, didn't you?"

"I took him to a place where they can't find him," Elsa said. "And if they can't find him, they can't find me."

They arrived at the eye clinic several minutes early, and while her grandmother went through the series of tests that always preceded an examination by the doctor, Elsa looked for something to read, but the magazines were all about sports or homemaking, so she sat and waited without any distraction from the thoughts that were swirling in her mind. They centered around immigration, and after a while they followed a direction that led back to the Dominican Republic.

She had just turned fifteen when her family made a visit to their home country. They stayed in Santa Cruz, at a small hotel that in season would be filled with tourists. An uncle of her father whose name was Eusebio lived in the town, but his house was in the *barrio* and didn't have room for them. In fact, it only had one bedroom and a main room that served as a living room, dining room, and kitchen. Its walls were made of assorted wood, and its roof was metal. It didn't have plumbing, but it did have electricity, which came from a wire Eusebio had strung to the power line that ran between two concrete poles.

Though Elsa had grown up in a poor area of Yonkers, she had left all that behind when her family moved to a better area, and she was shocked by the poverty she saw in the *barrio*. She couldn't imagine living like that. Yet Eusebio, who was an old man, seemed perfectly content there, and he pointed out with pride that he had replaced the dirt floor with tiles salvaged from the demolished hotel on the hill. He said he had everything he needed here, and he would never want to live in New York, with all the crime and the cold weather.

They went on a tour of the *barrio*, which had similar houses with wires strung to the power line like threads in a spider web. Bela, who was Eusebio's younger sister, led them to a house that was painted green, with a typical metal roof, and she told them that it was where she had raised her family.

"Is this where you were born?" Elsa asked her mother.

"Yes, and my brothers were born here too."

"Were they older or younger?"

"They were all older, and they all stayed here. I don't mean here in Santa Cruz, but here in this country. Two are in Santo Domingo, and the other lives in Santiago."

"How long did you live in this house?"

"I lived here until I married your father."

"How old were you then?"

"I was nineteen."

"Wow. You were only four years older than I am now, and you were married."

"People got married younger then."

"Where did you live after you got married?"

"We'll show you." Her mother led them down the street, which wasn't paved, and around the corner onto another street. They stopped in front of a house that was painted pink.

"You lived in a pink house?"

"It wasn't pink then," her mother said. "It was blue."

"Wasn't it green?" her father said.

"No, it was blue."

"Was I born here?" Elsa asked.

"Oh, yes," her mother said. "You arrived fourteen months after we got married."

"How long did we live here?"

"Until after your brother was born."

"I was born here?" Tirson asked in disbelief.

"Yes, you were born here, a few months before we went to New York."

"Was I the reason you went to New York?"

"There were a lot of reasons," her mother said, "but you and your sister were two of them."

The next day they drove in a rented car to the farm where her grandmother was born. It was a few miles off the highway that ran from Puerto Plata to Santiago.

The road climbed into the mountains, which were green with foliage. They passed hamlets alongside the road that all seemed to have a *colmado*, with people hanging out. In the hillside pastures were cows and goats.

"*Ya viene,*" her grandmother said.

Her father slowed the car and turned onto an unpaved road, which after a while was reduced to a pair of tire tracks with grass in the middle. Following directions from her grandmother, he entered a driveway and stopped in front of an unpainted shack.

"Does anyone live here?" her mother asked.

"Not that I know of," her grandmother said. "A nephew lived here until about five years ago, but he finally left and moved to Puerto Plata."

They got out of the car and walked to the shack. The door was open, so Elsa and her brother went in. The place was empty, except for the remains of cardboard boxes that were composting in the moist heat.

"How long did you live here?" she asked Bela, who had followed them into the house.

"Until I was fifteen. There were seven of us, so it was cramped."

"I don't believe that seven people lived in this house," her brother said.

"You don't have to believe it, but we did."

"When you left," Elsa asked, "where did you go?"

"I went to Santa Cruz, where I heard there was work."

"Did you find work there?"

"I found work cleaning houses, and that's what I did until I met your grandfather. We moved into the house I showed you, and that's where I lived until I went to New York."

"When was that?" Elsa asked, unable to remember exactly when Bela joined them.

"It was after your grandfather died. If that hadn't happened," Bela added, "I'd still be living in that house."

"Well, I'm sorry it happened, and I'm glad you're not living in that house alone."

"*Gracias, mi amor*. It's not good to live alone."

"Now, how many children did your parents have?" Tirson asked as if he still had trouble believing that seven people lived in this house.

"They had eight children, but only five lived beyond the age of three."

"So how did your parents feed all those children?"

"They grew corn and beans, and they traded corn for rice, so we had beans and rice. They also raised chickens, so we had eggs, and once in a while we roasted a chicken. But we never had meat, except on feast days when they roasted a pig at the *colmado*. My parents traded eggs for a piece of meat, which we all had to share."

"You never had hamburgers or French fries?"

"No, I didn't," Bela said. "I didn't know such things existed. And I don't have them now. They're not good for you."

"They taste good."

"And so does sugar."

After that exchange petered out, Elsa asked: "Where did you go to school?"

"They had a school in the nearest village. I didn't always make it to class, but I got through fifth grade. I learned to read and write and do arithmetic."

They lingered in the abandoned house for a while, and then they went out into the sunlight.

"Is there anything you miss about this place?"

"I miss my family," Bela said sadly. "And I miss the fresh air. But I don't miss the struggle to survive. There were times when we didn't even have rice and beans, and we had to go to bed hungry. You don't know what that's like."

"I don't," Elsa said, humbled.

"I'm done," her grandmother said, approaching from the hallway that was lined with examining rooms. "I just have to pay them."

"Is everything okay?"

"Yeah. Everything's okay, *gracias a Dios.*"

She got up and accompanied Bela to the counter, where Bela gave them twenty dollars for her co-pay, and then they headed out. It was after ten now, and Elsa had a counseling session at eleven, but she still had plenty of time.

As they headed toward the turnoff to the Saw Mill Parkway, she told Bela: "I was thinking about our visit to Santa Cruz when

I was fifteen. I remembered going to the house in the *barrio* where Mom was born, and then to the house where I was born, and then to the farm where you were born. We were all born there. We're all immigrants."

"Like everyone else in this country," her grandmother said.

"But they don't think of *themselves* as immigrants. They only think of *us* as immigrants."

"You know," Bela said after a moment, "in our home country we didn't think of ourselves as immigrants, though our ancestors came there from Europe and Africa. The Haitians were the immigrants. And we didn't want them in our country."

"Why didn't we want them in our country?"

"They were darker than we were. We called them *negros.*"

Elsa pondered this. "Are you saying that Americans are no more racist than we are?"

"They're no more racist, but they're more selfish because they're a rich country, and they can feed a lot of immigrants. We're a poor country, and we can't even feed our own people. So there *is* a difference."

"But why are people racist?"

"They need to look down on other people, and the easiest way to identify people to look down on is by the color of their skin. You don't have to look beyond their skin. You don't even have to think about it."

"So people are racist because it's easy?"

"It's the easiest thing in the world, which is why we're all racists. The hardest thing is to look beyond other people's skin and find what's there."

"And what would we find beyond their skin?"

"We'd find the spirit of the Lord, which lives in all of us."

"Bela," she said, deeply impressed, "how would you like to counsel a guy who hates other people because of the color of their skin?"

"I wouldn't," Bela told her. "That's *your* job. And you have the education for it. I didn't go beyond fifth grade."

Her appointment for the counseling session was at eleven, which gave her plenty of time to take her grandmother home and then drive to the campus. Since it was summer, with most students gone until fall, the counseling center was open by appointment only. During the summer the head of the center, who was also a member of the faculty, came into his office a few days a week to see students by appointment, review notes, and prepare reports. During the fall and spring semesters Elsa worked four hours a week at the center, split between Monday and Wednesday. She had made the appointment for today because it was one of her regular days at the center and also because for students in need of counseling it was the day after a weekend during which they might not have access to professional help.

The center was on the lower level of Main Hall between the cafeteria and the library and next to the nurse's office, which was closed for the summer. Since the head of the center wasn't there now, Elsa opened the door with her own key, turned on the light, and went into the small room the counselors used for meeting with students. She sat down at the desk and looked to see if there were any messages for her, and since there were none, she mentally prepared herself for the counseling session. It was with a girl who had taken her introduction to psychology course in the spring semester and had done very well. In fact, she was a straight-A student. Elsa remembered the girl clearly. Her name was Lucía, and from the way she spoke Spanish she was of Mexican origin. She had been a conscientious student, but at times she had displayed symptoms of anxiety, which wasn't unusual for students in today's world.

"Dr. Romero?" the girl said shyly, appearing in the doorway of the room.

"Hi, Lucía," Elsa said, rising. "Come on in."

Lucía ventured into the room while Elsa got up and went around the desk to the sitting area, where there were two comfortable chairs.

"Please sit down," she said, indicating one of the chairs.

Lucía lowered herself very carefully into the chair, using the armrests to control her descent. She wasn't heavy. In fact, she was a slight girl who couldn't have weighed much more than a hundred pounds. But she acted as if she was afraid of breaking the chair.

"How's your summer?" Elsa asked her after sitting down in the other chair.

The girl shrugged. "It's okay."

"Are you taking courses?"

"No. I'm working full time."

"Where do you work?"

"At a restaurant in Yonkers."

"What do you do?"

"I bring food and clear the tables."

"Do you live with your family?"

"I live with my mother. She's the only family I have in this country."

"Where do you live?"

"We live in South Yonkers. We have an apartment near St. Joseph's Hospital."

"What does your mother do?"

"She cleans houses," the girl said as if she appreciated what her mother did. "She used to work for a company, but now she has her own customers."

"Where do her customers live?"

"In Hastings, Dobbs Ferry, and Irvington."

"How does she get to their houses?"

"She takes the bus, and then she walks the rest of the way."

Though she was only providing basic information, the girl was emanating symptoms of anxiety. It usually took a while to find out the cause, if there was a cause. Some people were anxious for no apparent reason. But in this case Elsa had a feeling about the reason. "Is there something you're afraid of?"

"Yeah. There is," Lucía said with terror in her eyes. "I'm afraid of being deported."

"Tell me about your situation."

"I came here illegally with my mother when I was five. For all those years I felt safe because I was protected by DACA, but the president terminated the program, and I see in the news how they're rounding up people and deporting them."

"Has anyone from ICE contacted you?"

"No. But I heard they raided an apartment in Yonkers with no warning, and they treated the people like criminals just because they were here illegally."

"Are you sure they hadn't committed a crime?"

"I'm not sure. I don't know the people. But I know they're deporting people like me."

"They can't just deport you," Elsa said. "They have to follow a process. And in New York the police aren't helping them. Our state and city leaders don't agree with the federal policy. So you're relatively safe here."

"I don't feel safe."

"I understand. But no one in this world is completely safe. I mean, I'm an immigrant, and though I'm a U.S. citizen now, I still have occasional fears of being deported. But I live with my fears, and even though the present government is doing evil things, I still have faith in the essential goodness of this country."

"I did have faith," Lucía said, "but I don't any more. I feel like I don't belong in this country. But I don't belong in Mexico either. I haven't lived there since I was five."

"You *do* belong in this country. It was built by immigrants like you, and based on your academic performance, you have a lot to contribute to it."

"Well, if I keep worrying about being deported, I won't be able to concentrate on my courses."

"Have you gotten any legal advice?"

"No. We can't afford a lawyer."

"Do you go to church?"

"I don't go now."

"When you did go to church, where did you go?"

"I went to San Pedro with my mother."

"We have a community service at San Pedro that gives free

legal advice to immigrants, so you should go there and talk with our lawyer."

"I didn't know about this service."

"If you still went to church there, you'd know about it. Do you still pray?"

"I still do," the girl said with despair in her eyes, "but I don't pray as much as I used to."

"Then pray to Our Lady of Guadalupe, talk with our lawyer, and see me at the same time next Monday, okay?"

"Okay. *Gracias.*"

FOUR

WHEN HE WOKE up the next morning Karl didn't know where he
was. In the past week he had slept in a different place every night,
and he was completely disoriented. Was he in Ohio? Pennsylvania?
New Jersey? New York?

Rolling out of bed and sitting up, he saw a clue on the wall over
the head of the bed. It was a crucifix, with the corpus on it. Then
he remembered that he was staying in the guesthouse of a Catholic
college, whose name he didn't remember. Except that it was larger,
the crucifix was like the one that had hung on the wall over the
head of his parents' bed in Freiburg. He wondered if it was
hanging over their bed now in Boynton Beach.

Of course he didn't communicate much with his parents. They
were both disappointed in him for splitting with Linda, not only
because they believed that marriage was sacrosanct but also
because they loved Linda and felt she was a good influence on
him. In his defense, he pointed out that he and Linda were only
separated, not divorced, and that it was temporary. His parents
argued that with her in St. Paul, Minnesota and him on the road,
consorting with people who were a bad influence on him, they
weren't likely to get together. They advised him to move to St. Paul
and get a job there and live with his wife and children and forget
all this nonsense about making America white again.

He forced himself to a standing position and hobbled into the
bathroom where after peeing he looked in the mirror and saw a
man much older than he was, a tired man who needed a shave.
That was one thing they forgot to put on the grocery list: a razor.

He wandered into the kitchen and got the coffee out of the
refrigerator where Elsa had put it. The top of the bag was folded
over, with a piece of cellophane tape holding it down. He unpeeled
the tape and unfolded the top of the bag, but it was sealed. At first

he tried to pry it open but then he realized that you were supposed to cut it with scissors. After looking through a few drawers he found the scissors and cut the bag about an inch from the top. Since he was holding the bag tightly around its middle, coffee spilled out onto the counter and onto the floor. He cursed the people who sold coffee in bags like this. Why didn't they sell it in cans like Folgers?

It took him a while to figure out how to use the percolator, but once he had it on the stove he thought about food. He found the eggs in the refrigerator and took out two, along with the butter. He found a pan in a lower cabinet and put it on a burner. He then got the bread, which Elsa had set on top of the refrigerator, and he took out two slices. She had gotten white bread, as he had requested, instead of getting a multigrain bread like Linda bought because it was better for their health. In their last weeks together they had fought about everything, including the type of bread they should eat. As he put the slices of white bread into the toaster oven, he should have felt he had won that particular fight, but inexplicably he felt he had lost it.

A few minutes later he took out the toast and laid it on a plate and buttered it. He then put some butter into the pan and heated it. When it was ready, he cracked the eggs into the pan and cooked them for a while, then flipped them over with a spatula he had found in a drawer. By now he had found everything he needed to make fried eggs and toast.

Instead of eating at the kitchen table, he took his coffee and food into the living room, and while having breakfast he watched Fox News. He had noticed Elsa's reaction yesterday, and not wanting to get into an argument with her, he had turned off the television. But he couldn't understand why she and others like her refused to accept real news instead of the fake news they were given by the liberal media. Did the truth hurt?

There was nothing on Fox News about the girl who had been killed at the demonstration, and he began to wonder if it had really happened. Since he had been there, he knew that a shot was fired and that a gun landed on the pavement in front of him. But the police had hauled him away before he even had a chance to see what had happened, so it was possible that the shot hadn't hit anyone, and that the "murder" of a black girl was only a fiction in order to give the deep state an excuse for repressing the Patriots for a White America.

Except for one thing. If there hadn't been a murder, then why had Junior threatened him?

He had just finished cleaning up after breakfast when he heard a knock on the door. He was still in his briefs, and assuming it was Elsa, he asked her to wait for a second, he would be right there. But when, after pulling on his jeans, he opened the door and saw it was the nun from yesterday, he was thrown off balance.

"I hope it's not too early," she said with consideration. She was tall for a woman, and she looked like she was in good shape. Her eyes were hazel, and her skin was the color of coffee with milk. A simple wooden cross hung from a lanyard around her neck outside her shirt.

"No, I've been up for a while," he assured her.

"I'm checking to see if you're all right."

"Yeah, I'm all right." He was standing in the doorway as if to stop her from coming in.

"Do you have a minute?"

"Yeah, I guess."

Neither of them moved until he finally stepped aside and let her enter.

"I thought we could talk about what happened on Saturday."

"I'd rather not talk about it."

"But it might be good for you to talk about it," the sister said. "I mean, it must have been a traumatic experience."

"I've had worse experiences," he told her.

"I imagine you have, but this experience happened only two days ago."

For a while they stood and faced each other, as he and Elsa had faced each other at the demonstration, only neither of them had signs to convey their message. Then, remembering his manners, he said: "Would you like to sit down?"

"Yes, that would be nice." She moved toward a chair, allowing him to have the sofa.

"Okay," he said, feeling as if he was back in elementary school about to be scolded by Sister Hildegard for misbehaving. "What do you want to tell me?"

"I don't want to tell you anything. I want to know how you feel about what happened on Saturday. But before we go further, please don't think of me as a nun."

"How could I *not* think of you as a nun? You have it written all over you."

"You have experience with nuns?"

"I want to a Catholic school through eighth grade."

"So you're a Catholic."

"I *was* a Catholic, but I'm not anymore."

"What are you now?"

"I'm nothing," he said. "I mean, I have no religion other than my mission."

"And what's your mission?"

"You saw my sign. My mission is to make America white again."

She looked at him mildly. "Can you tell me why?"

"Yeah, I can tell you. I want to make our country like it was before the nonwhite immigrants came here."

"But it wasn't white before. There were brown people here before the white people came from Europe, and then a lot of black people were brought here from Africa."

"They don't count. It was white until recently."

"Okay. And how would you make it white again?"

"We'd secure our borders and not let any more nonwhite immigrants into our country."

"What about the nonwhite immigrants who are already here?"

"We'd get rid of them," he said, conscious of the fact that his statement included her. "We'd send them all back where they came from."

"That would be very hard on them."

"We don't care. They should have known they wouldn't be welcomed here."

The sister paused, and then she said: "Your ancestors must have been immigrants. If our country hadn't welcomed them, you wouldn't be here."

"That was different."

"Why was it different?"

"My ancestors were white."

"You mean white immigrants aren't a problem, but nonwhite immigrants *are* a problem."

"That's right."

"But whether they're white or nonwhite, the people who leave their home countries and come here only want a better life for their children."

"If they want a better life for their children," he said, recalling an argument he had heard, "then they should create it in their own countries. They shouldn't take it away from us."

"You've met Elsa. Her parents came here as immigrants from the Dominican Republic because they wanted a better life for their children. And they have a better life than they had in their home country. Did they take their better life away from you?"

"Well, they could be an exception. But most of the immigrants who come here are killers and rapists."

"Where did you get that idea?"

"It's not an idea, it's a fact."

"It's not a fact. The data show that immigrants commit crimes at a far lower level than the general population."

"That data is fake."

"So anything that doesn't agree with you is fake?"

"No, but it's a proven fact that immigrants commit almost all the crimes in our country. You see it on the news every day."

"Well, instead of watching the news on television, maybe you should do some research using that computer. You might learn something."

"That's what Elsa said. Is this a conspiracy?"

The sister smiled understandingly. "It's not a conspiracy. We only want to help you."

"Why should you want to help me?" he asked, though he knew

why. It was what their religion made them do.

"From what Elsa told me, you're in a bad situation."

"What do you know about my situation?"

"I know you have a dilemma. If you don't help the police catch the killer, he'll be free to threaten you, but if you do help them, you'll get into trouble with your group."

"I'm already in trouble with my group. They know I talked to the police, and they must think I told them who fired that shot."

"Do you know who fired that shot?"

He sighed. "You're the third person who's asked that question. And the answer is, I don't know, but I think I know."

"Did you tell the police what you think?"

"No. If I had, I'd be in even worse trouble with my group."

"So they're in favor of killing nonwhite people?"

"They're in favor of getting rid of nonwhite people, and killing them is one way."

The sister shook her head sadly. "I know you're not a Catholic anymore, but you don't have to be a Catholic to believe killing is wrong."

He sighed again. "Yeah, I believe killing is wrong."

"Then why do you hang out with people who believe it's right?"

"I agree with the other things they believe."

"Do the other things justify killing?"

"I don't know. I never thought about it before. I mean, they never killed before."

"So how do you feel about what happened on Saturday?"

"I have to admit," he said, opening up a little. "I was shocked by what happened. It's not at all what I expected when I joined the movement."

"You should have expected it," the sister told him. "Hatred leads to violence. So the question you need to answer is, why do you hate nonwhite immigrants?"

He felt as if she was giving him an assignment, and though he had long ago shed the influence of nuns in his life, he couldn't simply ignore her question. So after a long silence he said: "I'll think about it, sister."

For a long time after Sister Solana left the guesthouse he sat on the sofa, thinking about her question. He knew how it felt to hate people because he hated the assholes who had ruined the company with their financial games. But he didn't have that same feeling toward nonwhite immigrants. In fact, he didn't hate *them*. He hated what they were doing to his country. He hated losing his position of dominance as a white male.

Yet their conversation had revealed that he applied a double standard to immigrants. If they were white, they were good for the country, but if they were nonwhite, they were bad for it. And this double standard led him to another question: why did he feel that whites were better than nonwhites. Had he always felt that way? Had his parents felt that way? The problem was, in the all-white community where he and his parents had lived, there weren't any immediate questions about racial differences. Everyone was white, except for people you saw on television, and they were lovable idiots. They didn't pose a threat to his way of life because they had adopted the same way of life. They lived in suburban houses with their cars and their pets and their outdoor grills. The dangerous ones lived in New York and Chicago and Los Angeles, but who in his right mind would ever want to live in those cities?

So he wasn't entirely satisfied with his statement to the sister that the immigrants who were his ancestors weren't a problem because they were white. Was that really true? Were they accepted by the people who already lived in Ohio? Or were they regarded as unwelcome aliens who threatened those people's way of life? He had no answers to these questions because he had no information about his ancestors, other than family stories that didn't go back far enough.

Deciding to learn something, he got up and went to the computer and turned it on. He activated the browser, and using his two index fingers, he typed "German immigrants in America." And he was surprised by the number of items on this subject.

He started at the top, and worked his way down the list of sites. A major fact that he hadn't known was that there were more Americans of German descent than of any other nationality, including Irish. There were more than forty million of them. Yet at the beginning they were a minority. An early group was the Pennsylvania Dutch, who were German-speaking immigrants and their descendants. They were called "Dutch" because they spoke Deutsch, which meant German. Most immigrated from Germany or Switzerland in the seventeenth and eighteenth century. From Pennsylvania some of them migrated west to Ohio, and they were followed by a flood of German immigrants who typically arrived in Baltimore and travelled over land to the Ohio River, which transported them to Cincinnati. In the 1830s that city became a magnet for German immigrants, who established their own churches, clubs, and newspapers. Some of the older residents felt threatened by the Germans and blamed them for many of the city's problems. The strong anti-German sentiment led to the Cincinnati riots of 1855 in which a nativist mob tried to invade the German neighborhood. The Germans, in armed militia units, erected a barricade along the boundary between their neighborhood and the rest of the city, and after three days of fighting they finally repelled the mob.

Because there were so many German immigrants, with their different language and different customs, native-born Americans felt threatened by them. They believed that these foreigners would corrupt the morals of the country, and that the quality of life would decline because there were not enough jobs to employ all the German immigrants, so nativist movements arose and tried to limit immigration. But the flood of German immigrants to Ohio continued through the nineteenth century, and by the 1890s there was a major German presence in the state. The city of Cincinnati had three German morning newspapers and one German evening paper. German was taught in all the schools. Seventy churches held services completely or partly in German. There were more than a hundred German societies involved in mutual aid, athletics, trade unions, music, culture, and charity. They were gradually becoming an important group.

They had a major setback during World War I when Germans were persecuted and regarded with suspicion. The government prepared a list of German aliens and imprisoned many of them on grounds of spying or supporting the German war effort. A person with a German name was dragged from jail by a mob and lynched. Orchestras replaced German music with French music. In Cincinnati the public library removed all German books from its shelves. Streets and towns with German names were renamed. A few states prohibited the teaching of German in their schools. In response to this persecution many families of German descent Americanized their names (for example, changing Schmidt to Smith) and stopped speaking German in public places.

There was another period of persecution during World War II, but by then the process of assimilation had blurred most of the differences between descendants of German immigrants and descendants of people from other European countries. Most of them no longer read or spoke German, and many of them had intermarried with other groups.

As he did his research, Karl wondered why so many Germans had migrated to America, and pursuing the question, he learned that when the migration started there wasn't a nation of Germany, there was only a collection of kingdoms, principalities, duchies, and other such states, which warred with each other regularly, creating political instability. Investigating further, he learned that the main forces that drove Germans from their home states were economic, not political. Their states had become drastically overpopulated, and the local farms couldn't produce enough food for so many people. They left because if they had stayed, they would have starved, and they came to America because there was so much land available.

Sitting back from the computer, Karl thought about what he had learned. His ancestors hadn't been welcomed in America, and at times they were harshly persecuted, especially during World War I. They were white, but they were regarded with the same aversion as nonwhite immigrants today. So maybe it wasn't about being nonwhite. Maybe it was about being different. Maybe there was something in humans that made them fear people who were different, and fearing them led to hating them.

Karl imagined what it had been like for the founder of his family in America, who had arrived in Cincinnati during the early 1850s. For a while this man had done menial work, and then he had left the city to settle on a farm, which originally was fifty acres. He worked hard and did well on the farm, which his son expanded by another fifty acres. His son spoke English, but maybe he still had an accent from his parents, and when he went into town to sell his produce, how did they treat him? Did they talk about him behind his back using ethnic slurs? Did they call him names like Hun, or Boche, or Heinie, or Kraut?

He was awakened from an unpeaceful nap on the sofa by a knock on the door. He checked his watch, and saw that it was almost two in the afternoon. He had slept through the time when people on normal schedules had lunch.

He got up and went to the door and opened it.

"Hi," said Elsa with friendly smile.

"Hi. Come in." He stepped aside from the doorway.

"You look like you were having a nap."

"I was," he admitted. "I spent the morning on the computer, and it wore me out."

"Did you have breakfast and lunch?" she asked, coming into the living room.

"I had breakfast, but I didn't have lunch. The nap had priority."

"I could make you a tuna sandwich."

"No, thanks. I'm not hungry."

"So how are you doing?"

"I'm doing okay. I mean, I wish I didn't have to stay here, but I have no choice, so I'll have to make the best of it."

"Did you hear from the police?"

"No. But I turned off my phone right after I got that threat."

"I think you should turn it on for a moment to check and see if the detective called you."

"Why do you think he called me?"

"He called me," she told him, sitting down in the chair where the sister had sat. "He was checking to see if you're still in the area."

"Okay," he said. He had left his phone on the night table in the bedroom, so he went and got it and came back. He turned on his phone and saw a message from the detective asking him to return the call. Not wanting to risk using his phone, he turned it off.

"Was there a message?"

"Yeah. The detective asked me to return his call, but I don't want to use my phone."

"Then use the landline of the guesthouse."

"Okay." He moved toward the phone on the table. "I don't have his number."

"I have it in my phone," she told him, reaching into her pocketbook. She took out her phone and found the number and read it to him.

He called the number, and a woman answered. She asked him to wait a moment, and then the detective got on the line, saying: "Detective Ferraro."

"It's Karl Reinholdt."

"Thanks for calling. Are you still in the area?"

"Yeah. I'm still in the area."

"I wonder if you've remembered any further details that could help us in our investigation."

"I'm sorry, but I haven't."

"We tracked the itinerary of your group to a farm in New Jersey, and we're interviewing the people we found there. We're making a list of all the people in your group who came to New York for the demonstration."

"I gave you the names I knew."

"Yeah. But they were only first names. You didn't give us any last names."

"I don't know any last names," he insisted, though he did know one last name.

"In a day or so," the detective said, "I'll ask you to come back and talk with us. Maybe by then you'll remember more."

"Okay. Just call this number."

"What's wrong with your phone?"

"The battery's dead, and I don't have my charger."

"Well, stay in touch," the detective said.

"I will," he said. He ended the call and put the phone back in its cradle.

"Does he want you to go and talk with him?" Elsa asked.

"Not now, but he will in a day or so. They're interviewing people in our group."

"That's good." She got up, saying: "If you're not hungry, I am, so I'm going to make tuna sandwiches for both of us."

He didn't object. He followed her into the kitchen and sat down at the table. She was wearing loose fitting clothes, but the contours of her body could still be mapped.

"You said you spent the morning on the computer," she said, reaching for a can of tuna where she had placed it in a cupboard. "What did you learn?"

"I learned a lot. For one thing, I learned that there are more Americans of German descent than of any other nationality."

"Really? More than Irish?"

"There are more than forty million."

"That's a lot. There are only about two million Dominicans."

"I also learned that they came here mainly for economic reasons. They couldn't grow enough food in Germany to feed the population, so they came here, where they could get land and feed themselves."

"Well, the immigrants now come here mainly for economic reasons. They can't grow enough food in their countries to feed the population, so they come here, where they can get jobs and feed themselves."

"So nothing much has changed."

Opening the can of tuna, Elsa said: "One thing has changed. Your German ancestors were white, and the immigrants now are nonwhite."

"I hate to admit it," he said after a pause, "but I learned that it's not about being nonwhite. It's about being different. My ancestors were different, so they weren't welcomed, and at times they were harshly persecuted."

"That's interesting."

"It took several generations for people to accept them."

In a stainless-steel bowl she broke up the tuna with a fork. "Did you find out if there were movements like yours back then?"

"There were. There were movements that wanted to send the Germans back where they came from. They hated Germans, and they wanted to get rid of them."

Elsa got the mayonnaise out of refrigerator and brought it to the table. "So what did you conclude from your research?"

"I concluded that maybe there's something in humans that makes us fear people who are different, and fearing them leads to hating them."

She let go of the spoon she was using to take mayonnaise out of its jar, and she came over to him and gently patted his back, saying: "That's a very good insight."

For some reason, which he didn't understand, her praise meant a lot to him.

Sitting at the kitchen table, they drank beer with their sandwiches. She had insisted on having Presidente, so they both drank it, out of the bottles. Reluctantly, he admitted to her that it tasted better than Bud Light.

"In case you want to know how I spent my morning," she said while they were eating, "I took my grandmother to the eye doctor, and then I had a counseling session with a student."

"What's wrong with your grandmother's eyes?"

"There's nothing wrong with them, thanks to the doctor. She had a cataract removed and replaced with a lens, and now she can see with that eye. She thinks it's a miracle."

"That's what my mother would think."

"Is your mother religious?"

"Yeah, she is."

"Well, anyway, my grandmother's fine, and now she can enjoy the *telenovelas* more."

"What are *telenovelas*?"

"They're soap operas in Spanish. Most of them are made in Mexico."

"What about the student you counseled?" he asked after taking a long swig of beer.

"She's not fine. She's close to having a meltdown."

"What happened to her?" he asked.

"Nothing happened to her, but she's afraid of what might happen to her."

"What's she afraid of?"

"She's afraid of being deported."

"Deported? Is she an illegal immigrant?"

"Yeah. Her mother brought her to this country when she was five. Until recently she was protected by an executive order, but now she's exposed to the threat of deportation."

"Well, I can understand why you think she should be given amnesty. But if we give amnesty to people like her, then millions of people will come here expecting amnesty."

"They might, but if you listened to this poor girl, who was going to college and doing well until she was thrown into limbo, you wouldn't worry so much about that."

"Is there anything you can do to help her?"

"I can't do anything about her status. Only the government can do that. But I can help her deal with her situation."

"You can? How?"

"By giving her hope."

"So you have hope to give her?"

"I do. I believe that love will prevail."

"That's what your sign said."

"I carry that sign to every demonstration, and I totally believe what it says. Or I wouldn't carry it," she added.

He felt a wave of admiration for her, which prompted him to say: "If you can help her, then maybe you can help me."

"Maybe I can," she said, raising her green bottle of beer as if she was offering him a toast.

He clinked his bottle against hers.

FIVE

WHEN SHE LEFT the guesthouse Elsa started walking toward the convent, hoping to talk with Sister Solana and share their thoughts about the situation. She stopped for a moment and texted the sister, and then she continued. Within a few minutes she got a reply, suggesting they meet outside the front door of the convent. That was better than meeting inside because it was a hassle to gain admittance. It always made Elsa feel like she was being judged in some way.

Sister Solana had come to America with her parents from the Dominican Republic at the age of five, as Elsa had, but instead of living in Alto Manhattan, her family lived in the Bronx, and she went to the high school that was operated by the Sisters of the Redemption. In fact, her father eventually got a job as custodian of the high school, which enabled him to buy a nearby house for his wife and three children. Sister Solana was the youngest, and though she wasn't a wild child, no one could have predicted that she would end up being a nun. She went to college at St. Catherine and majored in business and got a job with a large corporation in Manhattan, to which she commuted on the subway. Within a few years she had a serious relationship with a guy whose family was also from the Dominican Republic, and she was planning to marry him when after leaving his apartment one night she was suddenly attacked by a gang. It was right in front of her fiancé's apartment, where they had spent the evening, so he heard her screams and came to her rescue. But just before the police arrived, a gang member knifed him, and he died on the street. Solana, whose name was Julia at the time, was devastated by the loss, and after several years of grieving she found solace in the convent.

Approaching the convent, Elsa saw the sister waiting for her outside the front door, and after a hug they decided to walk to a secluded spot that overlooked the river.

"I checked on him this morning," Sister Solana said as they followed the path around the athletic fields, where there was no activity except for the fruitless search for food by a pair of geese on the artificial turf. "I think we had a good conversation."

"What did you talk about?" Elsa asked.

"We talked about his mission to make America white again."

"Did he tell you why he's on that mission?"

"He believes that things were better in this country before nonwhite immigrants came here. He can't explain *why* they were better, but he believes they were."

"Well, he used the computer to do research on his German ancestors. For one thing, he found out that there are more Americans of German descent than of any other nationality."

"I thought there were more Irish."

"I did too. But I knew there weren't more Dominicans."

"If you lived in the Bronx, you'd think there were."

"He also found that his German ancestors weren't welcomed by the people who already lived in Ohio."

"I can understand that. New arrivals are never welcomed by the people who already live in a place. My parents weren't welcomed in our neighborhood. But now they're the people who already live there."

They climbed the steps that led up to the path that overlooked the river, and breathing more heavily, they stopped to rest and enjoy the view of the Palisades, which could have been the wall of a lost city.

"There were movements in the nineteenth century," Elsa continued, "that wanted to make America what it was before the Germans came. So what's happening now isn't new. The only thing that's new is that nonwhite immigrants have replaced Germans as the newcomers who are ruining the country."

"Does he understand that?"

"I think he does. He admitted that it's not about being nonwhite. It's about being different. And his ancestors were different, so they weren't welcomed."

"It's a major step for him to admit that."

"Yeah, it is. He concluded that maybe there's something in humans that makes us fear people who are different, and fearing them leads to hating them."

"He actually said that?"

"He actually did."

They walked along the path for a while, and when they came to a bench they sat down. It was the place where Elsa had come during her meltdown. She was sitting here when Sister Solana came along and joined her as if she could tell that something was wrong, though she didn't know Elsa at the time.

"Now, where do we go from here?" Sister Solana asked.

"I don't know. From our conversation today, I believe he's capable of thinking for himself, but at times he acts like he was brainwashed."

"I have the same feeling. At times he says things he must have gotten from that movement."

"Well, at least he's not in contact with them."

"But he still feels loyal to them."

"I know. We have to get him to break with the movement," Elsa said. "Unless he does, he won't tell the police who he thinks killed that girl."

"So how can we get him to break with the movement?"

"We have to get him to think more for himself. And we have to make him realize that they're using him."

"Yeah," Sister Solana said, nodding. "If we can make him realize that they were willing to let him take the rap for one of their members, then maybe he won't feel loyal to them."

"The detective told him that in a day or so he wants to talk with him again. By then we need to get him to break with the movement, or else he won't tell the police anything more."

"So we need to keep working on him."

Elsa remained on the bench after Sister Solana had left to walk back to the convent. She needed to be alone for a while to reflect on the events of the day.

The trip with her grandmother to see the eye doctor went well. She and her grandmother had some good conversations. She especially liked what her grandmother said about what we would find beyond the skin of other people. Would she find the spirit of the Lord beyond Karl's white skin? Would he find it beyond her brown skin?

The counseling session didn't go so well. The poor girl had a high level of anxiety, and there was an obvious reason for it. She was terrified of being deported. So the cause of her problem wasn't psychological, it was political, and Elsa didn't have the power to change the girl's situation. She had done her best to allay the girl's fears, but the only constructive thing she had done was to suggest talking with the lawyer at San Pedro, who had professional expertise and could advise her what to do. She hoped that by next Monday the girl would be feeling less anxious, but she would still have to live with the uncertainty about whether she would be allowed to remain in this country, and that was a lot to deal with for a girl her age.

The conversation with Karl went better. Through his research he connected with his immigrant ancestors, and he discovered that the people who already lived in this country had the same negative feelings about them as he had about the immigrants of today. He even made the breakthrough of realizing the problem wasn't about skin color, it was about whatever made a group of people different: race, language, culture, religion.

Thinking about what made her people different, she recalled her visit to the *barrio* in Santa Cruz. It had jogged her memory to see the house where she was born, but since she was only five when her family left their home country, there wasn't much in her memory. What stood out in particular was the sad image of her grandparents when they said goodbye to them.

From conversations with her family Elsa knew how her grandparents raised their children. They sent all four of them to school in the *barrio*, and Yesenia did so well that she was given the opportunity to go to high school in Puerto Plata, a half hour away by public bus. Since Bela was determined to see her daughter get a high school diploma, she made sure that Yesenia always did her homework, always wore a clean uniform, and always looked as good as girls who lived in better neighborhoods. This vigilance paid off, and when Yesenia graduated from high school she was hired by a company in the *zona franca* that assembled medical devices. The *zonas francas* were industrial parks created by the government where foreign companies could enjoy the benefits of cheap labor, tax incentives, and reasonably good communications. They mainly produced clothing, but they also produced a variety of other products, including jewelry, cigars, and leather goods as well as medical devices.

Yesenia performed well at her job, which involved coordinating shipments of components and final products, and her salary helped to support her family. While working for the company she met the man who would become her husband. His name was Omar, and his job was to maintain the machinery in the factory. Since he was handsome as well as ambitious, he was the prize that the young unmarried women aspired to win. In her telling of the story, while the other young women flaunted their physical endowments and flirted with him, Yesenia dressed conservatively and ignored him.

When he started making advances to her, she resisted him, and she held out until he finally offered her a proposal of marriage, which she accepted after making him wait a week for an answer. The wedding was in the local church, and the reception was held at the restaurant in the new hotel up on the hill, which gave them a special rate because Omar's brother worked there. That night they moved into the house that they had showed Elsa. They were renting it from a man who had built it on speculation, hoping to sell it, but he was happy to get the rent while Yesenia and Omar saved to buy it.

Elsa was born fourteen months after they were married, and Tirson was born two years later. But only a few months after his birth the company that employed Yesenia and Omar closed the factory, unable to compete with the cheaper labor provided by China. In fact, about half of the factories in the *zona franca* closed at that time, which left about a quarter of the town's population without jobs. With the help of Omar's brother, Jhonny, who worked in the kitchen at the hotel, they got jobs there, Yesenia cleaning rooms and Omar doing maintenance. They earned much less than at the factory, but at least they had jobs while many of their neighbors had no jobs at all.

The factory closings hit the *barrio* in Santa Cruz especially hard because the *zona franca* was the main employer of people who lived there, and because the government did very little to help them. Elsa learned about their hardships from Bela, who told her about neighbors who had nothing to eat, about men who resorted to stealing from houses in more affluent neighborhoods, about girls who sold their bodies to put bread on the table of their families, about babies who died of malnutrition. It was these stories that had inspired Elsa to write her dissertation about the effects of factory closings on people who depended on them.

Her parents, feeling lucky to have jobs, did what they could to help their neighbors, sharing what they had, but after a year the hotel was dealt a fatal blow. An American company bribed the government to allow it to build a power plant in the harbor, right next to the *barrio*. The houses on the land needed for the plant were cleared by the government, which claimed that the people who lived in them didn't have titles, and in their place a huge steam-powered generator was erected. It was not only noisy, it also used a low grade of fuel oil that produced black clouds of noxious smoke. Evidently by design, the prevailing wind blew the smoke into the *barrio*, and many people, especially babies, began to suffer from respiratory problems.

The hotel survived only one year after the power plant was built. Their guests complained about the noise, about the view of the harbor being ruined, and about the grit that seeped into their rooms and soiled their clothes. By the next season the hotel had virtually no reservations, and it closed, expecting to receive reparation from the government. So directly and indirectly about two hundred more jobs were lost.

By then Jhonny, who had watched the houses being bulldozed

and concluded that the plant would destroy the hotel, was in New York, working at a bodega that an uncle had started years ago. The uncle, who had done well, was willing to sponsor both brothers, but Omar, who hadn't imagined what the plant would do to the hotel, let his brother go first. Jhonny was single and didn't have a family to worry about, and if he did well in New York, then Omar would follow him, bringing his wife and children.

Elsa remembered her parents debating whether or not they should leave their home and go to New York. She had been old enough to understand what they were talking about, and though she couldn't recall their exact words, she could still hear their arguments and could still feel the anxiety she had felt then.

"We don't have any family there," her mother said.

"We have my brother and my uncle," her father said.

"We don't speak English."

"We can learn English. Jhonny did, and he's only been there for two years."

"Where will we live?"

"Jhonny says we can all fit into his apartment, at least until we get our own place."

"His apartment has only two bedrooms."

"It has a big living room where we can stay."

"How will we support ourselves?"

"I'll work at the bodega."

"Will that be enough?"

"If it's not enough, you can get a job. In Alto Manhattan there're a lot of businesses owned by Dominicans."

"But how will we get used to the cold?"

"We'll get used to it," her father said. "A million Dominicans have gotten used to it."

Gradually, her mother was persuaded, until she came to the most important question. "What about our parents?"

"If we do well, we can bring them there. But in the meantime they have jobs, and if they need money, we can send it to them."

At the end it was his confidence that persuaded her to go to New York, the same quality that had persuaded her to marry him.

It wasn't his looks, his charm, or his way with women. It was his confidence that he could do well at whatever he did.

By the time Elsa left the bench there were long rays of sunlight streaming toward her, leaving the Palisades in shadow. She walked to her car, and after a glance across the campus in the direction of the guesthouse, she headed home.

When she got there her brother was already home from his job in Manhattan, where he worked for a giant high-tech company. She had no idea what he did in his job, but they paid him well, and he enjoyed doing it. He could have afforded to have his own apartment in the city, but he preferred to stay with his family. No doubt he liked the advantages of living at home, which included having his mother do his laundry and cook his meals.

She ran into him in the upstairs hallway, coming from his bedroom in khaki shorts and a gray tee shirt. He didn't have to wear a suit to work, but he did have to wear presentable clothes, and as soon as he got home he shed them as if they were a mandatory uniform.

"Hey, Tirson," she said. "Can you do me a favor?"

"Maybe," he said. "What is it?"

"Do you have any shirts that you don't want?"

"Maybe. What do you need them for?"

"I need them for a homeless guy."

"Are you helping the homeless now?" He had lived through her missions, which had begun with her saving puppies and kittens at the animal shelter, and though he always supported her mission, he never went out of his way to join her.

"I'm helping one homeless person, who needs clean clothes."

"Well, let's see what I have," he said, turning to go back into his room. "Do you want dress shirts or tee shirts?"

"Tee shirts will do," she said, following him. She stood by while he opened a drawer of his bureau and rummaged in it.

He took out a navy-blue tee shirt and held it up for her to see. "What about this?"

"It would be fine. Are you sure you don't want it?"

"I have enough of them. I also have a black one you can have."

She received the shirts from him, and she thanked him.

"Do you need pants?"

"Yeah, I could use a pair."

He opened another drawer and took out a pair of old jeans. "You can have these. They're not worn out, but they're too faded. That's not cool."

From the jeans her students wore, it evidently wasn't cool. What was cool now was to have holes in your knees as if you were a pauper. "Okay. Thanks."

"So who's this homeless guy?" he asked, facing her.

"He's a guy I met at the demonstration."

"How did that go?"

"You didn't hear what happened?"

"No. What happened?"

"A girl was killed. She was shot by a lunatic on the other side. She was black, a Haitian."

"You think it was racially motivated?"

"I know it was. Whoever shot her was with a group of white nationalists. I almost saw it happen. I mean, it happened only about twenty feet away from me."

"If those guys were out there to kill nonwhite people," Tirson said with an unusual look of concern, "you're lucky they didn't shoot you."

"I hadn't thought about that," she said. It really hadn't entered her mind that she could have been a target of the shooting.

"You *should* think about it. You're risking your life at those demonstrations."

"I'm risking my life when I get into a car. If I get killed at a demonstration, at least it will be for a purpose."

"Well, I don't want to lose my sister."

"You say the nicest things to me," she said, smiling.

He punched her gently in the shoulder. "I love you, that's why. So stop risking your life at those demonstrations."

"Okay. I won't. And please don't mention this homeless guy to our parents."

"Why not? Is he a secret?"

"I just don't want them to know what I'm doing."

Tirson frowned. "I hope you're not in a relationship with him."

"I'm not in *that* kind of relationship."

"Then what kind is it?"

"I'm only trying to help him."

"You mean help him get back on his feet?"

"No, I'm trying to help him change the way he sees things."

"So he's on the other side?"

She nodded. "He's a white nationalist. At the demonstration he was standing across the street from me with a sign that said MAKE AMERICA WHITE AGAIN."

"Why do you want to help *him*?"

"He needs help."

"But why do you always have to help people? Why can't you let them help themselves?"

"I have to help them because they get into situations where they can't help themselves," she said, speaking from experience.

"Well, I don't think you should mess with him. If a member of his group killed a black girl, what makes you think he won't kill you?"

"He won't kill me."

"You think he won't, but how do you know?"

"I just know. So don't worry. And I think we're making progress with him."

"You're doing this with someone else? Now, let me guess. It's Sister Solana, isn't it."

"Yeah. We're working together."

"That's better than trying to do it by yourself, but I still don't think you should mess with him."

"I'll be careful," she promised. She put her free arm around him and hugged him, saying: "Thanks for the clothes."

At dinner that evening they talked about other things. Bela talked about her visit to the eye doctor, where they had treated her so well, and Tirson talked about his trip to Montauk, where he and his friends had gone fishing. Neither of them mentioned what Elsa had told them about the guy who had stayed at their home for one night, and her parents didn't ask about him, evidently assuming that he had gone back where he came from.

Before dinner she had texted her friend Gleny asking if she was free to meet for a drink later than evening, and they had arranged to meet at a bar near St. John's Hospital. Gleny, who was the same age as Elsa, had immigrated with her family when she was seven, but they agreed that since she came from Santo Domingo, her having lived two years less in America was compensated by her having lived longer in a big city. They had met in their freshman year of college and had maintained a close friendship since then. In fact, Gleny was the only person other than Sister Solana who knew exactly what had happened to Elsa before her meltdown in sophomore year.

They had majored in different programs, and they had grown up in different neighborhoods of Yonkers, but they both had Sister Solana as their mentor, and they both went into helping professions, with Elsa earning a doctorate in psychology and Gleny earning a doctorate in physical therapy. Gleny was now working at a clinic near the hospital, and since she was a junior member of her group, she had to cover two evenings a week at the clinic, treating patients who came there after work. Tonight was one of those evenings.

They met at a pub called The Rehab Room where most of the customers were employees or affiliates of the hospital, including occasionally a physician with a nurse or nursing assistant. The drinks were affordable, and the food was edible.

When Elsa arrived there Gleny was already sitting at the bar, with a glass of white wine in front of her. She got up, and they hugged each other.

Elsa sat down next to her and tried to get the bartender's attention.

"I ordered a burger," Gleny told her. "I hope you don't mind."

"No, I don't mind. I had dinner with my family."

Gleny still lived at home, which helped her pay off the student loans she had incurred in graduate school, but she couldn't have dinner at home when she worked evenings, so those evenings she had dinner here. Since she had to decompress for a while after work, she came here for that purpose as well. "I saw on the news what happened at the demonstration. Thanks for letting me know you were all right. I was worried about you."

"I was only about twenty feet from where it happened," Elsa said. "I didn't think about it at the time, but my brother pointed out that I could have been a target of the shooting."

"Thank God you weren't. Have the police caught the guy who did it?"

"As far as I know, they haven't caught him." After ordering a glass of white wine she told Gleny everything, beginning with her confrontation on Saturday with the guy in the red baseball cap and ending with her conversation that afternoon with Sister Solana. "So we're working on Karl to convince him that he should tell the police who he thinks killed that girl."

"Why hasn't he told them?"

"He still feels loyal to the movement."

Gleny shook her head, saying: "I don't understand why people surrender their minds to movements."

"I don't either," Elsa said. "But people surrender their minds to religions."

"I know they do. But we don't agree with everything the church tells us."

"Well, some people do. They surrender their minds to it."

"But why?" Gleny asked. "And why did this guy surrender his mind to a movement of white nationalists?"

"They must have filled some need in him."

"What do you know about him?"

"I know his ancestors were German immigrants who settled in Ohio. And I know he had a job in a factory that closed."

"So he lost his job?"

"Yeah, he did."

"And he blames nonwhite immigrants for the loss of his job?"

"He doesn't blame us for that," Elsa said. "He blames us for what we're doing to his country."

"What are we doing to *his* country?"

"We're making it nonwhite."

"*Dios mio*. If that's his problem, he's really fucked up."

"Yeah, along with all the other people who voted for that monster."

"Remember," Gleny said, receiving a plate with her hamburger and French fries from the bartender, "we had a monster who ruled our home country. Rafael Leónidas Trujillo Molina. He was a racist who hated himself for having African blood in him. When he got up in the morning he patted talcum powder on his face to make it look whiter. And he didn't kill just one Haitian, he killed thousands of them. But with the support of America, he stayed in power for thirty-one years."

"Well, I think if we give this monster enough time, the same thing will happen here."

"I think it will. So how can we stop it from happening here?"

"For a start, we can get Karl to change the way he sees things. We can make him realize that without immigrants he wouldn't have a country."

Gleny took a bite of her hamburger and chewed thoughtfully. "You believe you can do that?"

"I don't believe it. I only hope I can."

"And what if you can't?"

"If I can't, then the police might not catch the guy who killed that girl, and the guy might kill Karl."

"Why would the guy kill him?"

"To stop him from telling the police who killed that girl."

"But if the police catch that guy," Gleny said, "then Karl won't have to worry about him."

"I'm sure he understands that, but he doesn't want to tell the police about that guy."

"You think he doesn't care if the guy kills him?"

"I think he cares. If he didn't care, he wouldn't be hiding."

"Then he must see that it's in his own interest to tell the police everything he knows."

"I think he sees that," Elsa said, "but he also still feels loyal to the movement."

"That's how they do it," Gleny said after swallowing another bite of her hamburger. "They get you to do what they want out of loyalty, even if it goes against your own interests. That's how the monster in our home country did it."

"But we got rid of him."

"Yeah. He went too far. He abused the loyalty of some key people, and they finally turned on him."

"Well, maybe that's how we can get Karl to break with the movement," Elsa said, grasping this idea. "We make him realize that they're abusing his loyalty."

Gleny nodded. "Yeah, that's how you can do it."

She sipped her wine, still not seeing exactly how to do it but hoping she and Sister Solana would figure out how within the next day or so.

SIX

IN THE EARLY evening he was sitting on the sofa, watching Fox News. The commentator was expanding on the President's tweet that said there was blame on both sides for the death of the girl at the demonstration, and Karl was questioning that statement. Were the students in Elsa's group, who were demonstrating peacefully, responsible for Junior's act of violence? Did they incite him to shoot that black girl? Clearly, they didn't because Junior had planned before he went to the demonstration to kill a black. So who was telling the truth about it, the liberals who condemned the white nationalists, or the President who said there was blame on both sides? From what he had observed at the scene of the crime, Karl had to admit that the blame was on the side of his group, a member of which had acted out his hatred of nonwhites.

He was wondering what to do about dinner when there was a knock on the door. Almost guiltily he turned off the television, and he went to the door. It was Sister Solana, who stood there with a takeout container.

"I brought you some dinner," she said. "It's from the convent. I thought it would be better than a frozen pizza."

"Come in," he told her, stepping aside.

"I also brought some Dominican rum for you." She held up a paper bag as she entered the living room. She went and put the container and the bag on the kitchen table. "The food is cold, but you can warm it in the toaster oven."

"Thank you," he said.

"Have you ever had Dominican rum?"

"Yeah, I have," he said, remembering the rum that Elsa's father had given him.

"Then you know about it." She got a whiskey glass out of the cabinet, unscrewed the cap of the netted bottle, and poured some amber liquid into the glass. "My father drinks it without ice, which he says ruins the taste of it, but if you want ice, I'll get it for you."

"I'll have it without ice," he said, moving toward the table. He picked up the glass and took a sip. It was as smooth as expensive bourbon. "It's very good."

"My father says it's the best in the world."

That was what Elsa's father had said. He had to give them credit for being proud of their home country and its products. "Are you having a drink?"

"I don't drink rum, except occasionally in a Cuba Libre, but I'll drink a beer if you have it."

"I do. I have Dominican beer."

"What other kind is there?"

He went to the refrigerator and took out a green bottle, opened it, and asked: "Would you like a glass?"

"No, thanks. It's better from the bottle."

He watched as she raised the bottle, tilted it, and took a swig. He couldn't imagine a nun from his school drinking beer like this.

"So what have you been up to?" she asked after wiping her mouth with the back of her hand.

"Oh, nothing much. I did some research like you suggested."

"And what did you learn?"

"I learned that my ancestors, who were German immigrants, weren't welcomed by the people who were already here. Not because they were nonwhite," he explained, "but because they were different."

"Very good. At the time were there nativists who wanted to send your ancestors back where they came from?"

"Yeah, there were. So what's happening now isn't new."

"Can you imagine what it was like for them?"

"I try, but it's hard. It was long ago."

"I understand. It's hard to imagine what it was like for people long ago."

They drifted into the living room, where she took a chair and he took the sofa.

"Do you have an answer to the question I asked you?"

"Why do I hate nonwhite immigrants?"

"Yeah. Why do you hate them?"

He was conscious of repeating what he had told Elsa, and he wondered if the sister had already heard it. "I don't hate them. I only hate what they're doing to my country."

"What are they doing to your country?"

"They're making it nonwhite."

"Okay. So you don't hate Elsa, and you don't hate me, you only hate what we're doing to your country."

He thought about it. "I guess I don't hate what *you're* doing, I only hate what *they're* doing."

"You mean the immigrants you don't know."

"That's right," he said, reluctantly following her line of argument.

"Then the hatred's not in your heart," she told him, "it's only in your head."

He understood the implication: it was easier to change an idea in a person's head than a feeling in his heart.

"So you hate what nonwhite immigrants are doing to your country," she said, pursuing the issue.

"Yeah. I do. They're making it like a foreign country."

"It's not like it was."

"No. It's not."

"I understand," she said with empathy. "Can you tell me how you've been affected by this change?"

"Yeah. I've lost everything."

"What have you lost?"

"I lost my job."

"Where did you work?"

"I worked in a factory. I worked there for almost fifteen years, and then the factory closed and we all lost our jobs."

"Why did the factory close?"

"The family who owned the company for more than a hundred years sold it to a private equity firm, which flipped it to another private equity firm, leaving the company with a pile of debt that it couldn't pay. So the company was liquidated."

"How many employees did the company have?"

"About three thousand."

"That must have hurt the town."

"Yeah. It destroyed the town."

"Did you grow up there?"

"I was born and raised there. My father worked in the factory before me, and my mother also worked for the company. They retired before it went under, but they lost about half of their pensions."

"Do they still live in the town?"

"No, they live in Boynton Beach, Florida."

"So you haven't lost your parents."

"No, I haven't," he admitted.

"Do you have any brothers or sisters?"

"I have a sister. She's a nurse. She lives in St. Paul, Minnesota."

"So you haven't lost your sister."

"Okay. But I've lost my wife and children," he blurted out, no longer able to hold it back.

"I'm sorry," she said. "Tell me about it."

"There's not much to tell," he said. "When I lost my job, I lost all control of myself. I started drinking and behaving badly."

"You were angry."

"Yeah, I was angry."

"Were you angry at immigrants?"

"No. I wasn't. I'd never met an immigrant. I was angry at the assholes—excuse me, sister—who ruined a good company with their greed and their financial games."

"If that's what they did," the sister said, "then you had a valid reason to be angry."

"I know I did, but I took it out on the wrong people."

"You mean your wife and children."

"Yeah. So it's my fault that I lost them."

"Are you and your wife divorced?"

"No, we're separated."

"Then there's still hope for a reconciliation."

He sighed. "There's hope, but not much. They moved to St. Paul, and my wife has a good job there. She doesn't need me."

"Maybe she doesn't for economic reasons, but she probably does for other reasons."

"I don't know what other reasons there could be."

"There could be emotional reasons."

He shook his head, dismissing such reasons as only stuff that mattered to women.

The sister didn't contest the point. She took another swig of beer and said: "This movement that you belong to, Patriots for a White America. What do they do for you?"

"They give me a mission, a reason for living."

"Do you get from the movement what you got from your job?"

"No, but it's better than spending my life in bars. If I hadn't joined them, I'd be dead by now."

"I understand. But how is their mission going to help you?"

"It's going to bring my job back to this country."

"Was your job transferred to another country?"

"The jobs we lost were all transferred to other countries. The people who own the factories don't care about the workers. They only care about making money."

"Now, there we agree," the sister said. "But I don't see how the mission of your movement will bring your job back. Unless the government gives companies incentives to create and keep jobs in this country, the jobs that were transferred to other countries won't come back."

"How would you know?"

"I have a doctorate in economics, so I know how jobs are created and destroyed."

With sudden new respect for this woman, he asked: "Are you saying that our mission won't bring my job back?"

"That's what I'm saying. Your mission won't create jobs, it'll destroy them."

"How will it destroy them?"

"By undermining our economy, which depends on immigrants."

He thought about it, trying to find an argument against what she had said. "Immigrants come here and they don't work. They're all on welfare."

"They do work. They have the same unemployment rate as the general population, and they're not entitled to welfare, so if they don't work they have no income."

"I don't believe it."

"Those are data from the government. Not only that, but unlike the vultures who destroyed your company, immigrants create new companies. More than forty percent of our major companies were created by immigrants or children of immigrants."

Having no facts to refute this statement, he said nothing.

"So you're wasting your time with this movement, whose members don't care about you."

"Why do you say they don't care about me?"

"If they did, they would have told the police who killed that girl. They wouldn't let him threaten you. And you wouldn't be a captive," the sister added with a smile, "with two brown women who are trying to convert you to their way of thinking."

He returned her smile. "I don't mind you and Elsa, though I do mind being a captive."

"Then free yourself. I know why you won't tell the police what you know. It's not because you're afraid of what people in the movement might do to you. It's because you're afraid of losing what you get from the movement."

"Oh, I don't know about that," he said, not wanting to continue discussing this subject. She had stirred up feelings that he was reluctant to acknowledge even to himself.

As if she understood, she changed the subject. "Tell me about your wife and children."

"My wife's name is Linda, and my children's names are Holly and Justin."

"How old are your children?"

"Eleven and nine."

"How long have you and your wife been separated?"

"About a year."

"That's not long."

"Well, it seems long."

"What kind of work does your wife do?"

"She's a data analyst for an insurance company."

"Did she move to St. Paul because your sister lives there?"

"Yeah. My sister helped her find a job."

"Then if you went back to your wife and children, you'd go to St. Paul?"

"Yeah, I would. But my wife has no reason to take me back."

"She has at least two reasons."

"You mean our children?"

The sister nodded, raising her bottle for a last swig.

When she had left the guesthouse he went into the kitchen and opened the container she had brought. It was roast chicken, mashed potatoes, and carrots. It looked good, so he put it into the toaster oven. Deciding not to drink more rum, he got a bottle of beer out of the refrigerator and opened it. He still couldn't get over the way that nun had swigged beer. It was certainly a change from the time when he was taught by nuns in school, and he could see how he would have preferred having this nun as a teacher. Those nuns were nice women, but this one actually seemed to understand him, and she didn't seem to judge him.

He was around twelve when his father drove him out into the country to see what remained of the family farm. His uncle, his father's older brother, had tried to make a living from the farm but after the drought of 1988 he gave up and sold the land to an adjacent farmer who was expanding. The land was being used for a profitable purpose, but the house was abandoned, and the white paint on its clapboard walls was peeling badly, with almost as much wood showing as paint. The front steps were shaky, and the porch was sagging as his father led him into the house, opening a door that looked about to fall off its hinges. Inside, the house smelled of the rodents that had taken over from the humans.

There was no furniture, so his father had to tell him which empty spaces had been the living room, the dining room, and the kitchen. His father had grown up among six children, and most evenings after dinner they had sat in the living room and watched television, the signals of which came through an antenna. They always ate dinner together, sitting around a plank table and passing bowls around, family style. They ate well because they grew a lot of corn, some wheat, and some vegetables, and they raised cattle. They also had chickens, which provided eggs. His mother did the cooking, helped by his sisters as they got older.

Upstairs there were four bedrooms, three of which the children shared in pairs of the same sex. The bedroom that his father shared with an older brother was in the northeast corner, the coldest room in the house during winter. They had needed an extra blanket to keep warm at night. With only one bathroom for a family of eight, his father said, it was lucky that only three of them were females.

After giving him a tour of the house, his father took him out to the barn. Like the house it was in a state of disrepair, but it wasn't empty. It now provided a dumping place for old machinery, including a tractor and a mower. Before, it provided shelter for cattle and a loft for hay. It was where his father raised a calf that won second prize at the county fair, where one of his brothers broke a leg jumping from the loft. It was in the barn where Karl felt that his father really missed the farm, though he didn't regret leaving it. With six children in his generation there was no way they could all support themselves on a hundred acres, and since all but one of them wanted to leave and go to the city, there was no argument about who should take it over. His father left right after graduating from high school and moved to Freiburg and joined another brother in a room at a boarding house. He soon had a job working at the factory, where he made more money than he ever would have made on the farm.

He had been working there for about five years, still sharing a room with his brother, when he met the woman who would become his wife. She was in the office of personnel, and she had told his foreman that she wanted to see him. Going into her office in his grimy work clothes, he felt uneasy with this woman in a clean dress who looked and acted older than he was but was probably younger. He assumed that she had attended college or at least some kind of business school because she was working in an office, not in a factory. She even had a desk, behind which she was installed in a position of power.

"Mr. Reinholdt?" she said as if she wanted to make sure she was talking with the right man.

"Yeah," he said, standing in front of her and not knowing what to do with his hands.

"Please sit down, sir."

He sat down in one of the chairs that faced the desk.

Looking at papers that were spread on her desk, she said: "I just want to verify your record. It says your first name is Fredrik, and your middle name is Werner. Is that correct?"

"Yeah," he said.

"It says you've been working here since July 1, 1972. Is that correct?"

"Yeah," he said. He had stolen a look at her face, which behind her tortoise-shell glasses was pretty. She had wavy reddish hair, with green eyes and freckled skin.

"It says you're single. Is that correct?"

"Yeah," he said, conscious of having responded four times in a row with this monosyllable and wondering if she thought he was dumb.

"Are you still living at 17 Lincoln Avenue?"

"Yeah, I am." He would have liked to expand this answer but didn't know how.

"Is that a house or an apartment?"

"It's a boarding house."

She made a note. "You have Wilhelm and Louise Reinholdt listed as your beneficiaries. Is that still valid?"

"Yeah, it's still valid," he said, appropriating a word from her vocabulary.

"Okay," she said briskly, indicating that they were done.

"Well, you know all about me," he said on a sudden impulse. "Could you tell me *your* name?"

She pointed to a sign on her desk that said: "Mary Flanagan."

It made him feel that he hadn't been observant, and he got up from the chair abashed.

"I'm sorry," she said as if she sensed his discomfort. "That was rude of me. My only excuse is that you're the twentieth employee I've met with this morning."

"I accept your apology," he said, feeling better. And leaving her office, he started trying to find the courage to follow up with her.

Karl had heard this story many times, and his memory of how his parents met was a fusion of their two points of view. They agreed that his father had waited only one day before calling his mother, and that they had been married a year later at Our Lady of Peace, which his mother's family attended.

It turned out that his mother hadn't attended college but had earned a certificate at a business school which qualified her for a job in personnel. She kept her job until Karl was born, and she didn't work outside the home again until her two children were in school. In the meantime his parents bought a house in a good neighborhood and lived comfortably on the wages his father earned at the factory. When his mother returned to the workforce it wasn't because they needed the money but because they could use some extra money. She got her old job back, and she soon advanced to a higher level.

Karl had nothing but good memories of growing up, playing in the backyard, going to school, and having meals with his family. His parents weren't overly demonstrative, but they always made him feel they loved him, no matter what he did. And he didn't do anything that upset them. He had friends that they approved of, and he always came home in time for dinner. Though he wasn't as good a student as his sister, who was two years younger, he did well enough in school, and he was a natural athlete. His favorite sport was football, and since he could run fast, he played end and excelled at it. He wasn't a big hero at the high school, but he was respected and admired, especially when in his senior year he caught a long pass that won the championship for his team. His exploit caught the attention of the most beautiful girl in the school, who became his girlfriend. By the time he graduated from high school they were dating and they were planning ahead.

His mother wanted him to go to college, but no one in the family had ever gone to college, so it would be a major step. She believed he had the potential, and there was a branch of the state university in a nearby city, so he could live at home while attending classes. Still, he would need money for tuition and fees, and after failing to get an athletic scholarship, he got a part-time job at the factory to pay his way. Within a year the job became full time, and he dropped out of college, which was the first thing he ever did that upset his mother.

"If you want to be successful," she said, "you need to have a college degree."

"Dad's successful," he said, "and he only went to high school."

"At that time a high-school diploma was enough, but it's not enough now for most good jobs, and in the future it won't be enough for any good job."

"I have a job. I don't need to get another job."

"You have a job now, but if anything happens to the company, you won't have a job, and without a college degree you'll have trouble getting another job."

"Nothing's going to happen to the company. It's been around for more than a hundred years."

"You never know what's going to happen in the future," his mother told him, "so you need to be prepared for anything."

Looking back, he had to admit that his mother had been right. But how could he have anticipated what would happen to the company? Its business was booming, and every week they were hiring more people. So he kept working full time, and when Linda finished high school they got married. With the help of their parents they bought a house in the neighborhood where they had grown up. Within a year they had their first child, Holly, and within another two years they had their second child, Justin. There was no need for Linda to work outside the home, so she devoted her time to raising their children. At that point Karl had everything a man could want: a job, a family, a house, and two cars.

He finished eating the food that the nun had brought him, and he got up from the table, went into the kitchen, washed the container, dried it, and left it on the counter. He got another bottle of beer out of the refrigerator and went into the living room and turned on the television, which was set to Fox News. For the past year it had been his primary source of information about what was happening in the country, but right now he didn't feel like watching it. He felt like watching a baseball game, but they wouldn't have the Reds, so he settled for the Yankees, who were playing the Rays. The pitcher for the Yankees was brown, so he could have been a Dominican. There were a lot of Dominicans in major league baseball, and he wondered why. Was it because they had a lot of natural talent for the sport? Or was it because they focused on it.

Of course they were immigrants. They came to this country because they had special skills to contribute, and they made the game of baseball better. They drew fans, which raised attendance at the ballparks, and they paid taxes on what they earned, so they helped the economy in several ways. If they weren't allowed to come into the country, something would be lost. But for all that they contributed, they weren't white, and if they stayed and had children they would make the country less white.

He sipped his beer, reflecting on the conflict between the two sides on immigration. He saw how the issue was more complex than either side contended. If you let everyone come into the country, you would have chaos. But if you were too restrictive, you would lose what immigrants brought to this country.

On an impulse that had nothing to do with immigration, he got up and went to the landline phone. Except to call Detective Ferraro, he hadn't used it, not because he thought it wasn't safe but because there hadn't been any reason to use it. But now he had a reason to use it.

He dialed the number and waited while it rang.

"Hello?" It was his daughter's voice.

"Hi, Holly. It's Dad."

"Dad? Where are you?"

"I'm still on the assignment," he said. Because they didn't know what was going to happen with their marriage, he and Linda had agreed on the cover story that he was on an assignment for a company.

"When will we see you?"

"When I'm done with the assignment. Is your mother there?"

"Yeah. I'll get her. I love you, Dad."

"I love you too."

After a few minutes Linda got on the line, saying: "Karl? Where are you?"

"I'm in New York."

"What are you doing there?"

"I'm waiting for something to be resolved."

"I read about what happened at that demonstration. I hope you weren't involved in it."

"I wasn't involved in it," he assured her, "but I tried to stop it from getting worse, so I was questioned by the police."

"I hope you're not in trouble."

"I'm not in trouble. I mean, I'm not in trouble with the law. But since I was a witness, the police don't want me to leave the area, so I have to stay here for a few more days."

There was a silence at the other end, and finally Linda said: "Then where will you go?"

"I don't know. I only know I don't want to go to any more demonstrations."

"Well, that's something. The children miss you."

"I miss them. I don't understand how this happened to us. But I'm trying to understand, and I'm being helped by two women."

"Two women?" In her voice there was a note of alarm.

"Don't worry. One of them is a nun, and the other is a professor of psychology. They have no interest in me other than to change the way I see things."

"So they might help you."

"At least they won't hurt me. And guess what?"

"What?" Linda asked as if she might be ready for anything.

"They're not white. They're immigrants from the Dominican Republic."

"Immigrants? Where did you meet them?"

"At the demonstration. They were on the other side," he added unnecessarily.

There was another silence, and finally Linda said: "Well, this could be a good experience for you."

"It could be," he agreed.

When they ended the call he felt better. At least now he had more hope of saving his marriage.

He went into the bedroom and got out of his pants and turned off the light and slid under the covers of the bed. He was lying awake when his curiosity inexplicably became stronger than his fear of being tracked through his cell phone. He reached for his phone and turned it on. He heard the sound of a text message being received, and he clicked on the appropriate icon.

The message was from Junior, and it said: "You won't get away from me. I'll find you."

SEVEN

THE NEXT MORNING they got up in the usual order: Tirson who had to take an early train into the city, her parents who had to be in their office by eight thirty, and Elsa who had to be in her classroom by nine.

Elsa got up after her parents went downstairs to have breakfast. On weekdays they usually had fruit, a piece of bread, and coffee. Their office was within walking distance, on Palisade Avenue in the building that her father and her uncle had bought as their first investment in real estate. At the street level was the office of a real estate agent, a cousin of Elsa's, and at the next two levels were the offices of the family business. Though they could walk there, her parents drove there because after working in the office for a while, her father drove around and checked the markets, which were in different neighborhoods of Yonkers: Elm Street, McLean Avenue, Lake Avenue, and Palisade Avenue. He also occasionally checked the bodega, the original venture on South Broadway, which was now being managed by another cousin.

"There's coffee in the percolator," her mother told her as she entered the kitchen. Her mother and her father were on their feet, ready to leave.

"Okay," she said, still waking up.

"There's also some mango in that bowl."

"We have another shipment of mangos today," her father said. "But there won't be any more, so enjoy them while you can."

She gave each of her parents a hug and told them to have a good day.

Alone in the house, she poured herself a mug of coffee, put some mango and a piece of bread onto a plate, and sat down at the kitchen table. She reflected on the fact that her cousins, who were Jhonny's children, were all involved in the family business whereas she and Tirson were doing other things. As the older child, Elsa had set the direction for them, though not without the encouragement of their mother, who after her experience in their home country firmly believed in diversification.

Tirson had gotten a degree in business from St. Catherine, which their father had supported, but he hadn't understood why his son then pursued a master's degree in electronic engineering at Manhattan College. He had wanted his son eventually to participate in managing the family business, and he didn't see how a degree in electronic engineering would be helpful for that purpose. But at the same time he was glad that Tirson was doing so well, and he did see the advantages of having sources of income outside the family business.

Sipping her coffee, Elsa remembered the taxi ride from Santa Cruz to the Puerto Plata airport, the flight to New York, the chaotic scene at JFK where hundreds of Dominicans crowded around the exit from customs to greet the arrivals, the elation of spotting Jhonny among them, and the fitful ride through the city traffic, over a bridge, and up to Alto Manhattan. Jhonny lived on the third floor of an old building, in an apartment with two bedrooms. He gave one bedroom to Omar and Yesenia, and he sacrificed his own bedroom for Elsa and Tirson, sleeping on a pulldown bed in the living room. They actually didn't feel cramped because they had more room in that apartment than in their house in Santa Cruz, so it wasn't a difficult adjustment for them, and they ended up living there for more than a year.

In the meantime, her parents were working to acquire enough savings to afford their own apartment, Omar repairing cars and Yesenia cleaning houses. Jhonny, who worked in the bodega that their uncle owned, was earning more money than either of them, and after many long discussions he persuaded Omar to join him in the food business. Since they wanted to have their own bodega, they asked their uncle to help them start one. Their uncle was willing to help them, but he didn't want more competition in his neighborhood, so he suggested that they look for an opportunity in Yonkers, where a lot of Dominicans were moving because it was less densely populated than Alto Manhattan and the rents were lower. It took them several months to find a location on South Broadway that was occupied by an Italian vendor of fruits and vegetables who wanted to retire. With funding from their uncle they bought the business, took over the lease, and converted the store into a bodega.

When it was ready for operation they found apartments in the neighborhood with the space they needed and rents they could afford. Jhonny was still single, but by then he had a serious girlfriend, so he rented an apartment with two bedrooms, planning ahead. They moved there from Alto Manhattan near the end of June so that Elsa could finish her second year of school without interruption. She was sorry about leaving her friends, but she believed what her parents said about having a better life in Yonkers.

The bodega was successful, but it became clear that it didn't provide enough income to support two families with increasing needs, so the brothers acquired a grocery store on Elm Street and expanded it into a supermarket that was larger than a bodega but smaller than a typical American supermarket. For neighborhoods of immigrants, who mainly spoke Spanish, it was the ideal type of store. It was big enough to provide essentials beyond food, and people could walk there. Most important, if it was managed efficiently, it could offer affordable prices.

After the success of two more supermarkets, the one on McLean Avenue and the other on Lake Avenue, the brothers moved their families to North Yonkers, in the neighborhood around St. Brigid. They were among the first Dominicans to move into this neighborhood, which was mainly Irish and Italian. Elsa didn't remember encountering any hostility, though at the school it took her a while as a transfer student to break the ice. It was easier when she started high school at Sacred Heart, where there was more diversity, though there were tight little groups of girls who had gone to middle school together and acted as if they had all the friends they would ever need.

Compared with her classmates, Elsa navigated her way through high school with relatively few bad experiences. The school was co-educational, so you always had boys around, and they could be annoying, especially when they made suggestive remarks. After feeling the pain of two friends who had broken up with their boyfriends, she resolved not to get involved with a boy, and she made it through high school keeping this resolution, though she was exposed to more than one temptation.

Encouraged by her parents, she did well in school. She didn't get the highest marks in her class, but her grades and her test scores were high enough for her to get a scholarship at St. Catherine. Being the first in her family to go to college, she had made her parents very happy, and they celebrated her graduation with a party at the Polish Center, attended by more than seventy members of their family and their community. It was the high point of her life.

The course she was teaching today was the Junior Seminar, which met on Tuesdays and Thursdays from nine to twelve. It was the capstone course for the sixty credits of liberal arts that the state required for a bachelor's degree, and all the college's undergraduate students had to complete it. Elsa was asked to teach this course when she started teaching as an adjunct, having just completed her master's degree, and now as an assistant professor she taught it as part of her regular course load in the fall, spring, and summer semesters. At first she had also taught a psychology course in the summer, but now with all her other activities the junior seminar was the only course she taught in the summer.

The students who took this course in the summer were those who had put off taking it, those who resisted taking it, or those who had failed it, so she didn't have a class of enthusiastic students. The basic course material was the history of the Hudson River region, and she rarely had a student who admitted to liking history. But she had created additional material about current issues of peace and justice, which the students liked better than the history, and the main challenge was to get them to connect the past and the present.

Though not by design, her class was in a room whose windows faced out to the Hudson River, and since the class met in the morning the sun didn't shine into the room and overcome the air conditioning, it beamed across the water and lit up the Palisades like a golden curtain.

Elsa arrived in the classroom about ten minutes early, and she found a few students there, absorbed in their smartphones. They hadn't turned on the lights because it interfered with their screens, but at nine o'clock Elsa turned on the lights, saying: "Okay, guys. You need to put away the monkey toys and pay attention to each other in the real world."

By then there were eleven out of sixteen students present. While she was taking attendance two guys shuffled in, and the remaining three guys wandered in one at a time until the last one finally arrived. She marked him present, telling him: "You're ten minutes late."

"I was stuck in traffic," he told her.

"Where were you coming from?"

"Mount Vernon. The Saw Mill Parkway was all backed up."

"That happens," another guy said helpfully.

"Well, if it happens," she told the late student, "you should leave home ten minutes earlier."

"I will," he said as if he really meant it.

She put her attendance sheet away, noting that the five late students were all guys. It wasn't always guys who were late, but that was the pattern. Girls came to class on time, girls did their homework on time, and girls got better grades.

The students had two written assignments that were due today. One was about the reading assignment, which covered the establishment of New Netherland, the Dutch colony in what was now most of the tristate area of New York, New Jersey, and Connecticut. Her questions on the readings were designed to make the students think about what would have happened if something had been different. For today her question was, what if there had been sixteen million Native Americans in the region with weapons equivalent to the Dutch weapons? Would the Dutch have still been able to establish a colony?

Following her usual procedure, she assigned the students to teams with four students on a team, and they rearranged the tables and chairs so that were sitting face to face. She appointed a leader of each team and gave them about twenty minutes to discuss the question, present three arguments on each side, and make a decision. While the teams were working she wandered about the classroom, monitoring them and answering any questions they might have. It made her happy to see them talking with each other, looking at each other, and reacting to each other, instead of being absorbed in their smartphones. They were learning to interact face to face, and they were obviously enjoying it.

At the end of twenty minutes she called on the team leaders, one after another, to report their decisions and their supporting arguments. Of the four teams, only one decided that the Dutch would not have won against the Native Americans because the latter had the home field advantage. The other three teams decided that the Dutch would have won because they were smarter than the Native Americans.

"Why do you think the Dutch were smarter?" Elsa asked.

"They came from a higher civilization," Oscar said. He was a Latino, whose family had immigrated from Ecuador.

"You think the Europeans had a higher civilization than the Native Americans?"

"Yeah, they did. They had more advanced technology."

"What do the rest of you guys think?" she asked the class. They were a mix of races and cultures, with maybe three out of sixteen having pure European ancestry.

"The Dutch were smarter," Jennifer said.

"Why do you think the Dutch were smarter?"

"Because they had more money."

"So money is a measure of intelligence?"

"Yeah, smarter people have more money."

"In some cases," Miguel said. "But in other cases luckier people have more money."

"You mean people who are born with money," Stephanie said.

"I also mean people who are born with talent like athletes."

"You have to work hard to do well at sports," said Carlos, who played soccer.

"I know, but if you don't have the talent, it doesn't matter how hard you work."

The conversation continued, branching into areas that had little to do with the original question, but Elsa let them talk freely. They were interacting with each other, they were using their minds, they were learning.

The discussion in the second part of the class was about the assigned question on a current issue. For today the issue was immigration. The question was, what should we do about the eleven million illegal immigrants in our country?

Again, she gave the students twenty minutes to discuss the question as members of teams, and then she asked the leaders to report on their discussions.

The teams all leaned toward creating a pathway for these immigrants to become legal residents, but Nick dissented from his team's answer, saying: "I think we should deport them. They broke the law, which makes them criminals."

"Breaking a law," Tameka said, "doesn't make you a criminal. If it did, you'd be a criminal."

"I would be? Why?"

"Well, last week you got a ticket for going through a red light, so you broke a law."

"That's not the same as crossing a border illegally."

"It's breaking the law."

"It's really not about the law," Serena said. "It's about racism. If those illegal immigrants were white, they'd already be legal residents."

"I agree," Richard said. "We talked about racism last week, and I think there's a connection between the two issues."

"What's the connection?" Nick asked.

"We have a long history of racism in this country, and we also have a long history of not treating immigrants well. They go together."

María, who wore a gold cross on a chain around her neck, said: "If our country wasn't racist, we'd treat immigrants as the Bible says we should."

"What does the Bible say about immigrants?"

"It says we should be kind to immigrants because we were once immigrants."

"Where does it say that?"

"In both the Old and New Testaments."

"According to my religion," Abdullah said, "we're all immigrants. Wherever we came from and wherever we live, we're immigrants in this world."

"Well, I'm not an immigrant," Nick said.

"Your ancestors were," Tameka said.

"That doesn't make *me* an immigrant. Besides, my ancestors were legal immigrants."

"When did they come here?"

"A hundred years ago."

"So they weren't special. Anyone could come to this country back then."

"Not anyone," Richard said. "Chinese couldn't come to this country."

"Just because a thing is illegal," Serena said, "that doesn't make it wrong. I mean, it's illegal to do drugs."

"You don't think it's wrong to do drugs?" Nick asked.

"It depends on the situation. And you can say the same thing about immigration."

"I agree," Jennifer said. "The people who come here illegally are escaping from poverty and violence."

"They only want a better life for their children," Serena said.

"And we can't blame them for wanting a better life for their children," Tameka said. "My ancestors didn't come here voluntarily, but if they were in Africa now, they'd want to come here, and they should be allowed to come here."

"Well, let's try to summarize," Elsa said. "What should we do about the eleven million illegal immigrants in our country?"

"We should give them a way to become legal," Richard said.

Except for Nick, who maintained his position, the rest of the class agreed.

"Now, what about the wall? Should we build a wall on the border of Mexico?"

"What would be the point?" Oscar asked. "Whatever kind of wall you build, people could find a way to get over it."

"Or under it."

"They could dig a tunnel," Carlos said. "Like El Chapo did. Was that cool?"

"What happened to him anyway?"

"I think they caught him."

"Well, it was still cool what he did. He fooled everyone."

"Okay," Elsa said, redirecting them. "Are there any more thoughts about the wall?"

"Yeah," Richard said. "It would be a waste of taxpayers' money. And the president is just trying to buy votes from rednecks in the Midwest."

"They're not all rednecks," Nick said. "Some of them are people who lost their jobs to immigrants."

"The immigrants didn't take their jobs," Tameka said. "The immigrants are doing jobs that those people would never do."

"Then why did those people lose their jobs?"

"Because of globalization. Their jobs were outsourced to China."

"They also lost their jobs because of automation," Richard pointed out. "Their jobs were taken over by robots."

"That's why I'm majoring in marketing," Serena said. "Robots will never take over jobs in marketing."

"They already have," Jennifer said. "Who do you think is calling your parents to sell them windows or cleaning services?"

"That's not marketing, it's only sales."

"Okay," Elsa said. "Do we agree that the wall would be a waste of money?"

They all agreed, including Nick.

In the last part of the class a student had to do an oral presentation on a historic site. The assignment was to do research on the site and its historical importance, visit the site, and prepare slides on the material. It was Tameka's turn today, and she did her presentation on Philipse Manor Hall, a house in Yonkers that was built in 1682 by Frederick Philipse. He was an immigrant from the Netherlands who came to New Amsterdam with almost nothing but through hard work and a strategic marriage amassed a fortune and became one of the largest landowners in the colony. The current exhibit at the manor was on slavery, which was more widespread in New York than most people realized. In fact, Philipse told people that he made more money on the slave trade than on any of his other businesses, which included milling, commerce, and foreign trade in nonhuman goods.

Tameka did an excellent presentation. In addition to photos of the exhibit on slavery, she also showed photos of the manor and its spacious rooms, one of which had portraits of the first six presidents.. She ended with the fact that a descendant of Frederick Philipse made the mistake of siding with the British in our War of Independence and as a result lost all his property, including the manor and more than fifty thousand acres of land in what was now Westchester County.

She then invited the students to ask questions.

Oscar, the first to raise his hand, asked: "If this guy was a slave trader, and his family sided with the enemy, why should his house be a museum?"

"He played an important role in our history," Tameka said. "The manor is the oldest surviving house in Yonkers. And we need to be reminded that slavery existed in the North, not only in the South. In fact, slavery was financed by New York bankers."

Jennifer said: "I like the part about how George Washington visited the manor with the hope of marrying a Philipse girl. What would have happened if he'd married her?"

"The family might not have sided with the British."

"Or he might have sided with the family."

"I don't think he would have," Nick said. "He was a loyal American."

"He wasn't an American," Tameka pointed out. "He was a British subject. And from their point of view, he was a traitor."

The questions and responses continued, and they finally came back to the point that Frederick Philipse was an immigrant who did well.

"If they'd had laws against immigration back then," Richard speculated, "they might not have let him into the country."

"It was a colony, not a country," Miguel said, "but he was Dutch, so they would have let him into the colony."

"He wasn't Dutch, he was Bohemian," Tameka said. "His family fled to the Netherlands because they were being persecuted for their religion. But they let anyone into the colony. They didn't have laws against immigration."

"So if the English hadn't taken over the colony," Carlos said, "we wouldn't have an issue now with illegal immigrants."

Since time had run out, Elsa decided to end on that note. She told the class they had done a good job, and she reminded them to check the online learning system for the next assignments, which were due on Thursday.

From the classroom she went to the cafeteria, and when she got there she decided to get something for Karl. It was noon now, and he must be hungry. Also, he would probably welcome something other than a tuna salad sandwich.

As she moved along the counters she didn't see anything that appealed to her. It was summer, so the offerings were limited. Beyond the hot items was a counter where they would make you a sandwich to order. There were prepared sandwiches, but in her experience they were either dry or soggy, so she stopped and addressed the guy who was standing behind the counter: "Could you make an Italian wedge?"

"Yeah." He looked glad to have something to do. "What do you want on it?"

"Ham, salami, lettuce, and tomato."

"You want onion? Cheese?"

"No onion, but cheese."

"What kind?"

"Provolone."

"Oil and vinegar?"

"Yeah, no mayo."

"One foot or two feet?"

"Make it two feet. I'm sharing it." She didn't know why she told the guy she was sharing it. Was she worried that he would think she was an overeater?

She watched him make the sandwich. He was in his late twenties with dark eyes and dark skin and a white cap covering his hair. He looked and sounded like a Mexican. No doubt the food company that employed him paid him only the minimum wage, and tipping wasn't done in the cafeteria.

He wrapped the sandwich in paper and sliced it in half, then put it into a bag and handed it to her, saying: *"Disfrútalo."*

"Gracias. You live in Yonkers?"

"Yeah. I live on South Broadway."

"I used to live in that area. We had an apartment near McLean."

"We buy our food at a store on McLean."

"Is it a supermarket?"

"Yeah. I was hoping to get a job there, but they didn't have any openings."

She reached into her pocketbook and took out a business card and handed it to him. "Try again, and show them this card. It might help."

"I will," he said, looking at the card. *"Muchas gracias."*

"De nada. Buena suerte."

She paid the cashier and left the building and walked to the guesthouse, where she knocked on the door. It took a while, but she finally heard a sound behind the door.

"Elsa?" he called in an anxious voice.

"Yeah. It's me." She wondered who else it could be other than Sister Solana.

He opened the door, looking relieved to see her.

"Did something happen?"

"I'll tell you," he said, peering behind her as if to make sure that she hadn't been followed. After closing the door and locking it he said: "I got another text message."

"What did it say?"

"It said 'You won't get away from me. I'll find you.' "

"How would he find you?"

"I don't know, but he says he will."

"That's wishful thinking on his part. There's no way he could find you here."

"My phone isn't on, but I wonder if there's still a way he could track it."

"I don't know if there is," she said, taking her phone out of her pocketbook. "So I'll ask an expert."

"Who's that?" he asked.

"My brother. He's not an expert on phones, but he knows a lot about techie stuff." She handed Karl the bag.

"What's this?"

"It's our lunch. It's a wedge."

"A wedge?" He looked as if the word meant nothing to him.

"A submarine sandwich. What do you call it in Ohio?"

"A sub. I never heard it called a wedge."

"Well, let me call my brother," she said, going to her contacts and scrolling down. When she got to Tirson she clicked on him, hoping she would find him at work.

"Tirson Romero," he said in a garbled voice.

"It's Elsa," she said. "Are you eating lunch now?"

"Yeah, I'm eating a taco at my desk."

"I have a question. Is it possible to track a cell phone?"

"It's not only possible, it's done all the time."

"What if the phone is turned off?"

"It's still possible, but you can only track the phone to where it was turned off."

"Could an ordinary person track a phone?"

"Sure. They just need a tracking app, which is easy to get. In fact, they could download a free app."

"So anyone can do it?"

"Yeah, anyone can do it."

"Well, how can you stop people from tracking your phone?"

"You can take out the battery."

"That would stop anyone from tracking your phone?"

"It might not stop the police, the FBI, the CIA, the Russians, or the Chinese, but it would stop most people."

"If you did that, would your phone work when you put the battery back in?"

"Yeah. It would only have to boot up again."

"Thank you," she said, attributing a new value to her brother.

"Why do you want to know?" he asked. "Is someone trying to track you?"

"No," she said. "But it's good to know in case someone ever does try to track me."

"You mean like a guy who's stalking you?"

"Yeah. Well, enjoy your taco. I'll see you later."

She hung up the phone and told Karl: "To stop people from tracking your phone, you have to take out the battery."

"Turning it off isn't enough?"

"They can still track you to where you turned it off."

"So if I take out the battery, it'll stop anyone from tracking it?"

"It'll stop that guy," she said, assuming that he didn't belong to any of the categories that Tirson had mentioned.

"Okay. I'll take out the battery." Karl went to the table where he had left his phone and with some difficulty took out the battery. "You think the police know where I am?"

"They probably know. They're New York police."

"That makes them better than other police?"

"It makes them more experienced in dealing with terrorists."

With a look of recognition, he said: "I hadn't thought of it that way, but I guess that guy *is* a terrorist."

"Of course he's a terrorist," she said. "People who use violence for political purposes are terrorists, and I don't care which side they're on."

"Are you saying we were terrorists in Afghanistan and Iraq?"

"The men and women who fought there weren't, but the people who sent them there were terrorists."

He worked his jaw as if he was considering this.

"Come on," she said. "Let's have lunch."

He handed her the bag, and they went into the kitchen where

she got two plates out of the cabinet and put the two halves of the wedge on them.

Sitting at the table, she watched him take a bite. "You like it?"

"Yeah. It's like the subs we used to have for lunch at the factory."

"Did the company have a cafeteria?"

"Oh, yeah. But the food wasn't great. So at times we'd buy subs from a guy who parked his truck outside the entrance."

"You miss it," she said with empathy.

"I do. It was my whole life."

"But didn't you have a family?"

He nodded. "I had a wife and two children."

"What happened to them?"

"They left me. I mean, my children didn't leave me. My wife took them away with her."

"So you miss them too."

He gazed at her with tears forming in his pure blue eyes. "I really fucked up. You wouldn't believe how I fucked up."

"I'd believe it," she said. "You think you're the only one who ever fucked up?"

"But you never did."

"Oh, yeah, I did."

"I don't believe it."

"Why would I lie to you?"

"I don't know. But it's hard to believe that someone like you could fuck up."

"We all fuck up. We're all human. But we all don't recover from it, and based on what I've seen of you," she said gently, "you haven't recovered from it."

"I felt I recovered when I joined the movement."

"I understand. But how do you feel about them now?"

"I don't know. I don't have the same feeling about them that I had before."

"What do you think changed your feeling?"

"Killing that girl. That's what did it."

"Well, if that hadn't changed your feeling, nothing would have. But it did, so there's hope."

"Hope for what?"

"Hope that you'll recover."

He took another bite of the sandwich and chewed for a while. "I know what you and Sister Solana are trying to do. You're trying to make me break with the movement."

"We're trying to *help* you break with them."

"But why?" He was holding the sandwich in the air between the plate and his mouth.

"If you break with them," she told him, "then you have a chance of recovering."

"Yeah, but *why* are you trying to help me? I'm a white nationalist who wants to deport nonwhite immigrants."

"Do you want to deport me and Sister Solana?"

He shook his head. "I don't want to deport you and her, but I want to deport all the rest of them."

"Are you sure? I mean, if you really wanted to get rid of us, you wouldn't make any exceptions."

He raised the sandwich and took another bite of it.

"The thing is, you want to deport people you don't know, but you don't want to deport the only two nonwhite immigrants you *do* know. And what does that tell you?"

He chewed for a while, and then he said: "I guess it tells me I don't know what I'm doing."

"Exactly. You're thinking the way they wanted you to think, so they could abuse you."

"They didn't abuse me."

"Yeah, they abused you. They put you in the front row of that demonstration where you'd be blamed for whatever happened, and if I hadn't been there with my eyes on you, you'd be in jail now. You'd be their sacrificial lamb."

He chewed for a while longer. "Are you saying they set me up?"

"Yeah. They set you up. I mean, why did that gun land right in front of you? It wasn't by accident, and whoever threw it knew you'd pick it up."

"How could he have known that?"

"He knew you wouldn't use it. He knew you'd try to prevent anyone else from using it."

"But how could he have known that about me?"

"He knew you don't belong with them."

"Why don't I belong with them?"

"You're not like them."

"How am I not like them?"

"If you were like them, you wouldn't be sitting here at this table sharing a wedge with a brown woman who speaks Spanish as her first language."

He nodded with a smile of recognition. "No, I wouldn't be. I'd be hanging out with them talking about how you're ruining our country."

"So give yourself a chance to recover," she urged him. "Break with the movement and tell the police who you think did it. Then you can go back to your wife and children."

He swallowed the last bite of his sandwich and said: "I'll think about it."

She cleared the table, washed the plates, dried them, and put them away while he wandered into the living room and turned on the television. It was tuned to Fox News, but he quickly changed the channel to News12, which provided local news for the region. She paused to watch a story about a girl who had saved an elderly man from drowning in a boat accident on the river. The girl was an experienced swimmer, and her name was Martinez. From a glance at Karl's receptive face, Elsa knew she didn't have to point out that the man owed his life to an immigrant.

As she left him she said: "I enjoyed our lunch."

"I did too," he told her. "Let's do it again sometime."

EIGHT

ALONE, HE WENT back to the sofa and sat down, reflecting on their conversation. He could see Elsa's point about how they might have set him up, putting him in the front row and throwing the gun so that it landed within his reach. Being relatively new to the movement, he was expected to pay his dues. It had been that way at the factory, where in his first year he was assigned to jobs that no one else wanted. But as time went on and he was accepted by the foreman and his coworkers, he was assigned to better jobs. So that could happen in this situation.

But did he want to belong to a movement that had killed an innocent girl just to make a statement? They might not have supported what Junior planned to do, but they must know he had done it, and since he hadn't been apprehended they must be covering up for him. Not only that, they must be willing to let someone else take the rap.

The possibility was upsetting. If they were hanging him out to dry, then how could he go back to them? How could he remain loyal to people who would let him go to prison for something that one of them did? Of course, Junior was more extreme than most of them, but he represented their position on race. And he not only talked about getting rid of nonwhite people, he actually did something about it.

Karl bent over and closed his eyes, afraid of what would happen to him if he broke with the movement. It would leave him where he was before the movement saved him from going under. It would leave him with nothing to live for.

Not wanting to think about it, he reached for the remote and found the list of stations and looked for something that wouldn't be interrupted by commercials. He skipped the public channels and came to a movie channel. They were showing *Midway*, which he had seen as a teenager on a movie channel with his father. His mother and his sister didn't like war movies, so the two males had watched it together.

He engaged the channel, where by luck the movie hadn't begun yet, so he got up and went into the kitchen and got a bottle of Presidente, which made him think of Elsa and her father and Sister Solana, who had swigged beer like a champ. He returned to the sofa just in time, and he became engrossed in the movie. Those were the days, he thought, when right was right and wrong was wrong, and we went to war for a noble purpose.

Linda wanted to go to college, so in the fall after she graduated from high school she started taking courses at the branch of the state university where Karl had gone for one semester. That was in the fall of 2002, when they got married. In the spring she discovered that she was pregnant, so she didn't consider resuming college until their second child, Justin, started school. At the time they didn't need the money she could earn from working outside the home, and she didn't need to be at home while the children were at school, so her taking courses shouldn't have been a problem, but for some reason that he didn't understand, Karl resisted it. In fact, it was the issue of their first major argument.

"Why do you want to go back to college?" he asked her.

"I want to have the qualifications to get a job," she told him.

"But you don't need to get a job. We have enough money."

"I want to work for other reasons. With the kids in school, I don't have enough to do."

"Then it's for you, it's not for our family."

"If I have more to do, it'll be good for all of us."

"I don't see how. You'll be driving back and forth to the university, so who'll be here when the kids get home from school?"

"I'll be here. I'll take classes in the morning."

"When will you study?"

"I'll study at night, after they're asleep."

"Well, I don't see how it's going to work."

She gave him a penetrating look. "Are you sure you don't want me to go back to college because you dropped out?"

"That's not the reason," he said indignantly. "It's because I care about the children."

"So I don't care about the children?"

"You care about the children, but you sound like you care more about going back to college."

"Look," she said. "You have a job now, but we don't know what's going to happen in the future, and if anything happens to the company—"

He interrupted her, asking: "Have you been talking with my mother?"

"No, I haven't. You mean I couldn't possibly have a thought of my own?"

"I only meant that you sound like my mother."

"I'm not your mother, I'm your wife. And I want to contribute to our family. You know I wanted to go to college, and I put it off while I raised our children. But they're in school now, so I have an opportunity to do what I wanted."

"All right," he finally said. "If you think you can handle it, go ahead. But I don't want our children coming home from school to an empty house."

"They won't," she said. "Don't worry."

She had just completed her degree when the company went under. Though her college degree eventually helped her get a good job, there were no good jobs in Freiburg anymore, so she had to work as a waitress at the diner, which wasn't doing the business it used to. Her wages and tips together with his unemployment compensation enabled them to survive for a while, but with no medical coverage they were thrown into a hole when Justin broke an arm on the playground, and they began to miss mortgage payments. Karl found part-time work on a road project, but that ended with the summer, and though his unemployment benefits were extended for another six months, they weren't going to have enough income to make it through the winter.

After trying in vain to find a job, any kind of job, he began to spend his idle days in a local bar, which was one of the few businesses in the town that was flourishing. He arrived there after the children had gone to school and Linda had gone to work, and he left in time to get home by two thirty, when the children got home from school. He didn't always make it in time, but he was able to justify his lapses with the argument that Holly at ten and Justin at eight were old enough to be at home without supervision.

By then he had reached the point where he preferred being at the bar to being at home, where he got nothing but grief from Linda. Among the many things that bugged him was her insistence that he could always get a job at McDonald's. Actually, he had applied there and gone back repeatedly, but the jobs there were taken by hillbilly women who had migrated to Freiburg from eastern Ohio or from Kentucky, where things were even worse.

At the bar at least he could be among people, mostly men, who understood what he was going through. Almost all of them had worked for the company, and all of them had lost their jobs. They had all tried to find jobs, and none had been successful.

"The only jobs in this town are at the hospital," one of them said glumly.

"And at the funeral home," another one said.

"No, people can't afford to have funerals anymore."

"What do they do with the dead bodies?"

"They bury them in their back yards."

"That's against the law, isn't it?"

"It probably is. But you think you'll go to jail for burying your dad in your back yard?"

"We buried our dogs in our back yard."

"Well, that's how they treat us, like dogs."

"They treat us worse than we treat our dogs."

"Yeah, I got this letter from unemployment telling me I have to give them evidence that I'm looking for a job, or else they'll cut me off."

"They'll cut us all off in six months."

"So this is the last of it?"

"This is the last of it."

"My wife says we should get out of this fucking town and go somewhere else."

"That's what my wife says. But I don't know where the hell we could go."

"I hear it's better in Texas."

"Yeah, they have all that oil. But you think you could get a job on an oil rig?"

"I don't know. I don't know shit about oil rigs, but maybe I could learn about them."

"Forget Detroit. It's down and out."

"And forget Cleveland."

"What about Florida?"

"You want to work in an orange grove?"

"You couldn't get a job in an orange grove. Those jobs are all taken by spics."

"What about a cotton field?"

There was laughter.

"Forget it. Even niggers won't work in cotton fields anymore."

"So what the fuck are we going to do? I missed two payments on my mortgage, and the bank is threatening foreclosure."

"Let them have your house. It's not worth shit."

"Yeah, who would ever buy a house in this fucking town?"

"This fucking town is dead, and if we don't get out of here, we'll be dead."

He lingered in the bar later and later, not wanting to go home. And when he finally did get home, Linda was waiting for him with guns blazing. She acted as if it was all his fault that he was unemployed, and that he was unable to find a job. She acted as if he was ruining their family by spending his days at a bar.

When they reached the point where they had nothing but her income to live on, she gave him an ultimatum. If he didn't find a job within two months, she was going to leave town and take the children with her. She had been applying for jobs in St. Paul, where his sister lived and had a good job at a hospital. According to his sister, the economy in Minnesota was doing fine, and it was easy to find a job there.

The ultimatum was probably the worst thing she could have done. It made him feel that she only valued him for the income he had always provided, and now that he wasn't providing it, he wasn't worth shit. His reaction was to stay even later at the bar, to drink more, and to come home drunk. By then he wasn't coming home for dinner, and by the time he did come home the children were in bed.

One night, while they were standing in the kitchen, they got into an argument that went too far. It started with her asking: "What's happening to you?"

"What do you mean?"

"You come home late, you come home drunk. You should see yourself."

"I see myself. I look in the mirror in the morning."

"What do you see? Bloodshot eyes?"

"I see a man who can't get a job."

"You can get a job. But you won't settle for anything but your old job. And that job won't come back."

"It *will* come back."

"It won't come back. We're living in a different world now."

"Well, I don't like this world," he said.

"I don't like it either," she said, "but I have to adapt to it, and so do you."

"I don't want to adapt to it. I want the world I had before."

"You sound like Justin when he loses a toy."

"I don't sound like Justin. I sound like all the men at the bar. We all want our old jobs back."

"Well, you're not going to get your old jobs back, so you better start training for new jobs. Before it's too late."

"Too late?"

"Yeah. The longer you hang out at that bar moaning about how you lost your jobs, the harder it'll be for you to recover."

"So what am I supposed to do?"

"You could take a course at the community college."

"A course in what?"

"A course in computers."

"Oh, I don't like computers."

"I don't care if you don't like them. You think I like being a waitress?"

"I don't know. I never heard you say you don't like it."

"That's because I don't complain about it."

"Well, I'll think of something."

"You don't have much time. We got another letter from the bank. They're starting the process of foreclosure."

He grabbed the letter from her, saying: "The fucking bank. They just suck money out of the community."

"If we lose our house," she said, "I'm leaving this town, with or without you."

"But you grew up in this town. Why do you want to leave it?"

"Because this town is dead, and I don't want our children to grow up here."

"Okay," he said feeling as if she had plunged a dagger into his heart. "You can leave without me. You don't give a damn about me. You only married me for my income, and now that I don't have any income, you treat me like a piece of shit."

"I don't treat you like a piece of shit. I treat you like a man who needs to get over losing a job that he expected to have for life."

"I had a right to expect that. My father had his job for life."

"That was yesterday's world," she said. "In today's world you don't have a right to a job for life. You have a responsibility to adapt to a different situation."

He should have listened to this, but instead he rejected it because he felt she was rejecting him, and it made him angry. It made him not only angry at her, but angry at everything, and he acted out his rage by picking up a glass from the table and hurling it against the cabinet door, from which it rebounded onto the floor, breaking into pieces. Not stopping there, he cleared the table, hurling the glasses and plates against the cabinet.

The noise eventually brought the children to the kitchen doorway, where they gazed at the scene with eyes filled with fear.

She left town without him. With the help of her brother she filled a rented trailer with clothes and furniture, and set off for St.

Paul. He stood in the street and watched the back of the trailer until it disappeared around the corner. He felt utterly abandoned.

Instead of waiting for the bank to complete the process of foreclosure, he walked into the local branch and gave them the keys to the house, which at that point had a market value that was less than the mortgage. He found a room in the house of a cousin, who didn't charge him rent because he was family. He supported himself by working in the stockroom of the supermarket, which was struggling to stay in business. He did the nightshift after spending the day at the bar. He was lucky that his supervisor didn't mind that he was never sober.

About two months after leaving with the children Linda wrote him a letter informing him that she had a job as a data analyst with an insurance company. The job paid well, and she suggested that he join her in St. Paul, where after some training he could get a job. He was tempted to go and join her, but something primeval deep inside of him resisted her suggestion, and he texted her, saying: "I'm not leaving Freiburg. My family has lived in this county for seven generations, so I have a right to live here. And I have a right to my old job."

He had missed most of the movie, but his attention returned to the television screen in time to see the American planes destroy a Japanese aircraft carrier. At the sight of the smoke billowing from the damaged ship, he felt like cheering. Those were the days.

He rubbed his eyes and got up from the sofa. It was after four, and he had nothing to look forward to but a long evening alone in this house with nothing to do and no one to talk with. He didn't expect to see Elsa again that day, and he didn't know if the nun would drop by. In any case, he didn't want to depend on their company. He wondered if there was a bar in the vicinity that he could walk to. He hadn't paid much attention to his surroundings while Elsa had driven to the campus because his mind was occupied by the threatening message. But now, with the battery out of his phone, he felt secure enough to venture outside and see what he could find in the neighborhood.

He followed a walk that led to the entrance of the campus, passing an old mansion that looked as if it had belonged to a very rich family. The family, out of guilt for having all that money, must have donated the mansion to the college along with the property. At the main street he passed a few students coming his way, with their eyes glued to smartphones. Somehow they managed not to run into him, as if they were bats with radar in their brains.

He walked down the street, and seeing ahead a large complex of buildings that looked like a hospital, he turned into a side street, which led him to a street that ran parallel to the street that ran by the campus, and there he saw stores: a pizza place, a pharmacy, a supermarket, and finally a bar called Hogan's.

Upon entering it he could tell right away that it was his type of bar. It smelled of beer and male sweat and urinal soap. There were no women in the place, and because it was early, there was still an empty stool at the bar. He sidled up onto the stool and tried to catch the eye of the bartender, a big man with tattoos on his arms.

"What'll you have?" the bartender asked him.

"I'll have a Jameson, no ice."

The bartender looked at him approvingly. "You got it."

He glanced at the guys on his left and his right. They were both in work clothes, and they were both about his age.

"Hey, man," the guy on the right said. "I haven't seen you here before."

"I haven't been here before. I'm not from Yonkers."

"Where are you from?"

"A town in Ohio."

"It's not Cleveland, is it?"

"No, it's a town near Cincinnati."

"The reason I asked is I got a sister who lives in Cleveland. She's an Indians fan."

"I'm not an Indians fan, I'm a Reds fan."

"My condolences," the bartender said.

"Are you visiting family?" the guy asked.

"No, I'm here on business."

"What kind of business?"

"I meant I'm here looking for a job. There aren't any jobs in the town where I live."

"What happened to the jobs there?"

"The main employer closed its factory."

"Aw, that's a bummer," the bartender said. "I bet the owners took their money and ran."

"Yeah, they did. They left us with nothing."

"That's what owners always do," the guy on the left said. "They fuck the workers."

"Well, now we have a president who won't fuck the workers," the guy on the right said.

"If you believe that, you're really gullible. That shithead never worked a day in his life. He has no idea what it's like for us."

"He's going to bring the jobs back. Just wait and see."

"Have people in this city lost jobs?" Karl asked.

"It's been slow because of the recession," the bartender said, "but we're okay. We don't have factories."

"We used to have factories," the guy on the left said, "but not anymore. They all moved south and then to China."

"Where do you work?"

"I work for the electric company."

"I'm a plumber," the guy on the right said.

"I worked in a factory that made components for auto bodies," Karl said. "They're making them in Mexico now."

"The president will fix that."

"Yeah, sure," the guy on the left said. "He won't fix anything. He only shits on Mexicans."

"Well, I don't like to hear people shitting on Mexicans," the bartender said. "If we didn't have Mexicans, our whole economy would collapse. They work in kitchens, they work in construction, they work in landscaping, they work in hospitals. They work their fucking asses off."

"I wasn't shitting on them," Karl said. "I just said they're making our components in Mexico and not in Ohio."

"Then you have a legitimate grievance, but most people who shit on Mexicans have no reason to talk that way. In fact, they benefit from Mexicans."

"Are you Mexican?" the guy on the right asked jokingly.

"No, but if I was, I'd be proud of it. Just like I'm proud of being Irish. You know, there was a time when people were shitting on the Irish."

"I know they were," the guy on the left said. "They treated the Irish like a lower form of life."

"And now you have to be Irish," the guy on the right said, "to get a job with the electric company."

"That's a crock of shit. We even have Italians working there."

The guy on the right, who was evidently Italian, said: "They're the ones who do the work."

"No, they're the ones who always say we're not doing a job correctly."

"The chances are, you're not doing the job correctly. Whenever I pass one of your work sites, I see about eight guys standing around and watching a guy who's down in the hole. And he's the Italian."

"Whatever he is," the guy on the left said, "he's the low man on the totem pole."

"If you're looking for work," the guy on the right said, "you have a good chance of finding it here. If you're Irish, you can get a job with the electric company."

"I'm not Irish," Karl said. "I'm German."

"Well, that's okay. We have a lot of Germans."

"We have a lot of everything."

"I assume you have mechanical skills."

"I know how to operate machinery."

"You know how to fix it?"

"I can fix some kinds of machinery, but I'm not a mechanic."

"You know what he should get into," the bartender said. "Heating and cooling."

"That's a big business."

"It is," the guy on the left said, "especially with the climate change."

"There's no such thing as climate change," the guy on his right said. "That's a hoax."

"Next time you look at your electric bill, tell me it's a hoax."

"I don't look at my electric bill. My wife handles all the bills."

"You trust her with your money?"

"Yeah, I trust her. She's better with money than I am."

"You mean she doesn't spend it in bars."

"Speak for yourself."

At that moment someone tapped Karl on the shoulder. He jumped as if he thought it might be Junior, but when he turned his head he saw it was Sister Solana.

"What are *you* doing here?" he asked her, feeling that nuns shouldn't be in bars, especially this type of bar.

Smiling, she said: "I came here thinking you might be here."

Not wanting to talk with her in front of his companions, he looked around and saw an empty booth. "Let's go and sit in that booth, okay?"

"Okay," she said, turning.

"What do I owe you?" he asked the bartender.

"Don't worry. I'll run a tab for you. Just let me know what the sister wants."

"You know her?" he asked, surprised.

"Yeah, she comes here now and then with another nun. They sit in a booth and have long conversations."

He took his drink and went over to the booth and asked: "Can I get you a drink?"

"Yeah, you can get me a white wine," the sister said.

He got it for her and had his own drink replenished at the same time. He set the glass of white wine in front of her and then sat down.

"I dropped by the guesthouse," she told him. "I knocked on the door and I called to you. When you didn't respond, I was worried about you, so I used the extra key and went inside and looked around. I was glad I didn't find you there."

"You mean you thought I might have killed myself?"

"No. I thought they might have found you and killed you."

"They won't find me," he assured her. "With the help of Elsa's brother, I fixed my phone so they can't track me."

"Well, since I didn't find a body, I figured you'd gone out, and my first thought was that maybe you'd come here."

"Why here?"

"It's the only bar in the neighborhood."

"But why a bar?"

"Where else would you go?"

He nodded, saying: "You know me."

"I don't know you, but I know men like you."

"How do you know them? From hanging out in bars?"

"No, from working at a homeless shelter."

"So you think I'm homeless?"

"You are, aren't you?"

He took a slug of Jameson. "Yeah. I *am* homeless. I have a room at a cousin's house in Freiburg, but I don't live there."

"Your wife has a home in St. Paul."

"I know, but after what I did, I could never go back to her."

The sister looked at him closely. "Last night you said your wife had no reason to take you back, but now you say that after what you did, you could never go back to her, which tells me you think she *would* take you back."

"She probably would. She even invited me to join her."

"Then she's not the problem, you're the problem."

"I know I am," he said, annoyed by her perception. "I don't need a nun to tell me that."

"The first time we met," the sister said, "I asked you not to think of me as a nun."

"But how could I *not* think of you as a nun?"

"By opening your mind. That's your problem—your mind is closed. It's not open to new ways of living. You think the only way to live is the way you lived before they closed the factory. But there are other ways of living."

"What do you know? You live in a convent."

"I haven't lived there all my life."

"I never would have guessed."

"There you go again. You see a nun and you think she joined the convent when she was eighteen and never did anything else."

"So what else did you do?"

"I worked in the finance department of a corporation."

"You're kidding."

"I'm not. And I was very good at my job."

"Then why did you leave it?"

She paused and took another sip of wine. "I won't bore you with the whole story, but I met a guy and we fell in love. We were planning to get married, and suddenly I lost him."

"How did you lose him?"

"I was leaving his apartment one night, I was going home, and I was attacked by a gang. I hadn't gone far from his building, so he heard my screams, and he ran down to save me. He did save me, but just before the police arrived they killed him."

"Oh, no," he said, feeling for her.

"I went into a meltdown, like you did. My family couldn't help me, my friends couldn't help me, no one could help me—until I met a nun who could help me. And that's why I became a nun. I wanted to help people in trouble."

He reflected for a while, and then he said: "So you know what it's like to lose the most important thing in the world."

"I lost a human being, who couldn't be replaced. You only lost a job, which could be replaced in many ways. And you haven't lost your wife and children, who *should* be the most important things in the world."

"I guess I'm beginning to realize that."

"Then get over losing your job, and go back to your wife and children."

"I would, but—" He hesitated. "I'm so ashamed of what I did."

"Get over that too. It's only your pride, and you know what pride is? It's a deadly sin."

"If it's a sin," he said, still resisting, "I have to be forgiven."

"If you're sorry," she said, "you *will* be forgiven."

"You mean God will forgive me."

"God will always forgive you, but you have to give humans a chance to forgive you. So give your wife a chance to forgive you."

He nodded, saying: "I'll think about it."

They walked back to the campus together.

They came to the guesthouse first, so they parted there. He never could have imagined what he did then. He put his arms around the nun and hugged her, and she reciprocated, holding him as tightly as he held her.

Outside the door of the guesthouse he watched her walk the rest of the way to the convent, where she would lie in bed alone and remember the man she had planned to marry.

NINE

LEAVING THE CAMPUS, Elsa drove south on Broadway and over to Warburton Avenue. She had an appointment at three with a student who was trying to learn English in a program sponsored by San Pedro. The student, whose name was Melany, had come from El Salvador with her daughter seeking asylum from the violence there. Her husband had been tortured and killed by a gang, and her father had paid for her transportation through Mexico and over the border, where she had been detained, processed, and released pending a court appearance, which was scheduled for November. In the meantime she was living with a brother in Yonkers, not far from the church. She was twenty-two, and her daughter was six.

Elsa passed Main Street and continued south on Riverdale Avenue until she arrived at San Pedro, where she met with Melany on Tuesday and Thursday afternoons. She pulled into the parking lot, where she saw Arlen, the man who ran the church's food pantry. He was taking delivery of food from her family's stores, which were important donors. It was her mother's idea to give back to the community in this way.

After getting out of her car she said hi to Arlen, but she didn't stop to talk with him because he was busy. She went into the basement of the church, which was occupied mainly by the food pantry, but there was a section for immigrant services that included legal, economic, and language assistance. Her student was waiting for her in the reception area. In the morning she cleaned houses, working for a company that was willing to employ women who didn't have papers. Melany was about the same shade of brown as Elsa, though her color and features came from Native American sources instead of African. She was also shorter and solider.

They hugged each other and went into a classroom that was designed for individual learning. It was just big enough for a table and two chairs.

The approach that Elsa used for teaching was to use English as much as possible and resort to Spanish only when necessary. She assigned readings to her students, from which they learned vocabulary, sentence structure, and idioms. She always began the class by asking students how they were doing.

"Estoy muy preocupada," Melany said, resorting to Spanish right away.

"What are you worried about," Elsa asked, though she could easily imagine.

"I heard that the ICE are going to apartments and taking people and deporting them."

"They are, but you're in a legal process, so they can't just take you and deport you."

"How do you know? I heard that they're not following the process."

"You have a lawyer who can make them follow the process."

"What if he can't? What if they separate me and Blanca?"

"They won't separate mothers and children. That would be a crime against humanity."

"Well, what if they send us back to El Salvador? We'll be killed there by the gang."

"They could send you back there," Elsa said, "but it's not very likely. If you follow the process and show up for your court appearance, you should be okay."

"I pray every hour of every day to the Blessed Mother that we'll be okay. But at times I lose faith, especially when I hear what they're doing to people."

"I understand. They shouldn't make you go through this. They're heartless. But don't worry. They won't be running our country for long."

"If we wouldn't be killed in El Salvador, I'd rather be there. I don't feel like I belong here."

"It takes time. You've only been here for three months."

"Yeah, I know," Melany sighed. "And after all we went through to get here, I guess we're lucky to be alive."

"So let's talk about the reading," Elsa said. "Tell me about it, in English."

As she listened to this young woman struggling to speak English, her heart went out to her. Elsa had been five when she started learning English, and it had been difficult even at that age, but it was much more difficult for Melany, especially since she was physically tired from cleaning houses and mentally tired from worrying about her daughter.

They worked on vocabulary and on prepositions, which in English were challenging for people who spoke other languages.

When they were done Elsa asked: "Would it help if we prayed together?"

"Yeah, it would," Melany said, her eyes brightening.

Elsa led the prayer, saying: *"Dios te salve, María, llena eres de gracia. El Señor es contigo."*

Melany joined her, and they said it together.

As usual, Elsa gave her student a ride home. It wasn't far, but she could imagine what it was like for Melany, whose daughter would be coming home from school, needing love and comfort. Elsa remembered coming home from school at the same age, needing love and comfort, and she understood now what it had been like for her mother who after cleaning houses since eight in the morning had to provide what her daughter needed.

On the way home she stayed on Warburton Avenue, passing the house where she had made the worst mistake of her whole life. She wondered if it was still being rented by students who wanted to live off campus. It probably was because there were three cars in the driveway and there was a recycling bin at the curb filled with empty bottles.

It was early March in her sophomore year at college, and she was having lunch with Gleny in the cafeteria. They had a morning class together which ended at 11:25 and their next classes didn't begin until 1:15, so they had plenty of time to eat and hang out. They were at a table that had four chairs, and they were engrossed in a conversation when they were interrupted by a guy who said: "Do you mind if we sit at this table?"

Elsa looked up, and what she saw made her heart thump. With his wavy blond hair and sparkling blue eyes and charming smile, the guy could have been a movie star. She had never seen such an attractive guy up close.

"There are other tables where you could sit," Gleny told him.

"But we wouldn't be with *you*," the guy said smoothly.

Despite not being welcomed by Gleny, the guys sat down and introduced themselves. The blond guy said: "I'm Bruce, and this is Larry."

Uncertain what to do, Elsa glanced at her friend to see if they should reciprocate and disclose their names, and Gleny shook her head.

"Are you guys from the DR," Bruce asked them.

"Yeah," Gleny said with caution. "So what?"

"So I've been there, and I love that country. It has the best beer in the world."

"Where did you go?"

"Punta Cana."

"That's not the DR, it's for tourists who want to enjoy our climate and our beaches without having to leave their countries."

"I flew there on JetBlue. So how can you say I didn't leave my country?"

"What you get in those resorts," Gleny said, "is what you get at home. You don't get anything Dominican."

"The beer is Dominican."

"And so's the rum," Larry said.

"But that's about all. The food you eat at those restaurants is imported."

"Well, I don't care. We had a blast there, and we're going back for spring break."

"Have a good time," Gleny told them.

"What about you?" Bruce asked Elsa. "You haven't said a word."

Rattled by his attention, she said: "I've never been to Punta Cana, so I don't have an opinion."

"You should go there sometime." He said this as if he assumed she had the money and the time to go there. "Where are you from in the DR?"

"Santa Cruz."

"Where's that?"

"It's on the north coast, near Puerto Plata."

"Oh, I know Puerto Plata. We almost went there, but people said Punta Cana was better."

"I wouldn't know," Elsa said.

"Are you in a dorm?"

"No, I live with my family."

"In Yonkers?"

Gleny shook her head, warning her, but she didn't see how it would hurt to say: "Yeah."

"Where in Yonkers?"

"On Broadway." That was a safe answer because Broadway went all the way from the city to Tarrytown and even farther, for all she knew.

"We live on Warburton Avenue. We're renting an apartment, four of us."

"It's a great place for parties," Larry said.

"We're not party girls," Gleny said.

"I know," Bruce said. "You're serious students. What are your majors?"

"Health science," Gleny said.

"What about you?"

"Psychology."

"That's a very good major. There're a lot of people with mental disorders who need help." Bruce paused and then said: "I'm majoring in marketing. I graduate in two months, and I have a job with a big corporation in the city."

"Good for you," Gleny said, unimpressed.

Bruce smiled at her. "You said that the food at Punta Cana

wasn't Dominican. Are there places in Yonkers where we can get Dominican food?"

"Yeah, there are several. You could try going to Caridad."

"Where's that?"

"On Broadway, south of St. Joseph's Hospital."

"I don't know that hospital. Where is it?"

"It's south of Main Street."

"Is it a safe area?" Larry asked.

Gleny laughed. "It's not like Punta Cana, if that's what you mean. But it's safe enough."

"Would you go there with us?"

"You don't think you could find it by yourselves?"

"I just think it would be more fun if we were with people who know what to order."

"There are a lot of Dominicans at this college," Gleny said, rising from the table. "You should be able to find someone who can help you."

With conflicting feelings Elsa got up and went with her friend, who headed for the bins where you disposed of trash. They still had time before their next class, so they wandered out to the terrace that overlooked the athletic fields.

"Why don't you want to go with them?" Elsa asked.

"I don't like them," Gleny said.

"Why don't you like them?"

"They don't respect us. They think they're better than we are."

"Well, I didn't get that impression at all. I thought Bruce was very nice."

"He's acting nice because he wants something from you."

"What does he want?"

"He wants to get into your pants."

"But how do you know?"

"From the way he looked at you. I mean, he put on a wonderful act, but there's only one thing he wants from you, and if he gets it, he'll dump you like a piece of shit."

She weighed her friend's opinion against her own, and she came out in favor of Bruce. "I think you're wrong. I think he only wants to go and have Dominican food with us."

"You like him, don't you," Gleny said, looking at her with concern.

"I don't know him, but from what I've seen of him, yeah, I like him. And I don't see how we could get into trouble by going to a restaurant with them."

"What if I refuse to go with you? Would you go without me?"

Based on her feeling, she said: "I might. But I'd rather have you with me."

"Then we'll go to Caridad with them. But that's it."

They went the next day, which was a Friday. They met in the lounge next to the cafeteria and walked to Bruce's car, which was parked in an area reserved for visitors. The car was a sport utility vehicle, and the girls got in back with the guys in front.

They headed south on Broadway, with Gleny giving Bruce directions. When they got to the other side of Main Street, Larry asked: "Are you sure this is a safe area?"

"We live in this area," Gleny lied. In fact, they had both lived in this area before their fathers did well enough to move to better areas.

"You do? Wow," Larry said, impressed.

The restaurant had a parking lot, which Gleny directed Bruce to turn into. They got out of the car, and she led them into the restaurant.

When she had lived not far from here, Elsa had come here with her family for special occasions, and they still came here now and then. To the left was a line of steam trays where people got takeout food, and to the right were booths with service. The waiters were playful Mexican guys who interacted well with the customers.

Gleny selected a booth, and the girls seated themselves on one side with the guys on the other. When their waiter asked if they would like drinks, Bruce said: "Of course. I'll have a Presidente, *bien fria.*"

"He speaks Spanish," Gleny said wryly.

"The only words I know are *cerveza* and *bien fria,*" Bruce admitted.

"But they go a long way," Larry said.

The guys ordered beers, the girls ordered sodas, and while they waited for their drinks they looked at the menus.

"What would you recommend?" Bruce asked.

"If you like pork," Gleny told him, "you should have the leg of pork with beans and rice and ripe plantains."

"That sounds good."

"I'll have that too," Larry said.

The girls decided to have chicken, and when the waiter brought their drinks Gleny ordered for them, speaking in Spanish.

"You speak so fast," Bruce told her.

"It only sounds fast because you don't understand it. When I first heard English, I thought people were speaking fast."

"How long have you lived here?"

"Since I was seven."

"What about you?" he asked Elsa, turning his blue eyes on her.

"Since I was five."

"Why did your families come here?"

"They came here to have a better life," Gleny said, "just like your ancestors did."

"Yeah, I guess that's why everyone comes here. I mean, if they didn't expect to have a better life here, they wouldn't have left their home countries."

She liked him for understanding that. It suggested that Gleny could be wrong about him.

The guys really enjoyed the food, as evidenced by their not leaving a single grain of rice on their plates. For dessert they ordered a flan to share. And when the waiter brought the check, they offered to pay it.

"We'll split it," Gleny said.

"But we asked you to bring us here," Bruce said.

"That doesn't mean you have to pay for us. We're not your dates."

Bruce yielded graciously, and they split the check. They went out to the parking lot, where Gleny said: "You don't have to take us home. We can walk from here."

"Are you sure?" Bruce asked.

"Yeah, don't worry. We won't be assaulted by a gang."

"Okay. Well, goodbye. We enjoyed the food."

Elsa started walking with her friend, but after they were out of hearing distance she asked: "I understand why you didn't want them to take us home, but how are we going to get there?"

"We can take the bus," Gleny said. "It stops across the street."

"You've taken it from here?"

"Yeah. Remember, I used to work here."

"Oh, yeah." She should have remembered, but her mind wasn't working properly.

They crossed the street and Gleny examined the time table. They would only have to wait for ten minutes.

While they waited for the bus they talked about Bruce.

"I think he's nice," Elsa said.

"I still think he's putting on an act," Gleny said.

"I liked him for saying why everyone comes to this country. It made me feel that he doesn't think he's better than we are."

"It was supposed to make you feel that way."

"Oh, I don't believe it was calculated."

"It's all calculated. They tell us they love our country, and they tell us they love our beer and our food, and they finally tell us they love us."

"Why are you being so cynical?"

"I know what guys are capable of doing," Gleny said. "A guy like Bruce convinced my cousin that he loved her, and she let him have sex with her. He knocked her up, and then he denied that he even knew her."

"What happened to her?"

"She had the baby, and she's living at home with her family, so she's okay now. But for a long time she was down at the bottom of a deep hole."

"Well, I don't think Bruce would knock up a girl and deny that he knew her."

"You don't know what that guy would do, so don't get involved with him."

"Don't worry. I'm not planning to get involved with him."

"That's good," Gleny said, putting an around her.

The next day she was coming out of a classroom when she saw Bruce standing in the hall, evidently waiting for her.

"I had to see you," he told her with a look of desperation.

"How did you know I was in this class?"

"I got someone to find out your schedule."

"Why did you have to see me?"

"I just had to. I was hoping to get your phone number yesterday, but your friend cut me off before I could get it. Why was she so hostile?"

"She had a bad experience."

"She did? Well, that's not my fault."

"I know it's not." She was conscious of the fact that in less than fifteen minutes she had to get to another class.

"Will you give me your number?" he asked with a vulnerability that touched her.

"Sure," she said after a moment. She gave it to him, watching him key it into his phone. And then she said: "I have another class, so I have to go now."

"Okay. I'll send you a message."

As required by the professor, she shut off her phone during the class, but when she turned it on afterward she saw a message from him. It said: "I would like to take you to dinner tonight, just the two of us. I can pick you up at six thirty. Just tell me where."

She was halfway home, walking south on Broadway, before she responded, accepting his invitation and giving him the address of her home.

She found her mother in the kitchen, preparing dinner.

"I won't be home for dinner," she said. "I'm going out with someone."

Her mother looked up from the counter, where she was cutting up a chicken. "You didn't say it was Gleny, so it must be someone else."

"It's a guy I met at the college."

"You mean it's a date?"

"I guess it is," she said. "He's taking me to dinner."

"Where's he taking you?"

"I don't know, but I'm sure it's somewhere nice."

"Is he picking you up?"

"Yeah. He has a car."

"Then we'll have a chance to meet him."

"Yeah. You will."

She changed her mind several times about what to wear, but she finally decided to wear her black pants and her blue top. She didn't have the kind of clothes that revealed cleavage or accentuated her butt, and even if she'd had them she wouldn't have worn them tonight. She was mindful of what her friend had said, and she didn't want to give this guy any wrong ideas. She was a virgin, and she intended to remain a virgin until she was married.

She was in the living room with her parents when the doorbell rang. She jumped up and went to the door and opened it. He was holding a bouquet of yellow roses, which he offered to her. Not knowing what to do with them, she said: "Thanks. Come in and meet my parents."

She led him into the living room, saying: "Mom, Dad, this is Bruce."

Her father rose to shake his hand. "It's a pleasure to meet you."

"Same here," Bruce said. He leaned over to shake hands with her mother. "I'm glad to meet you, Mrs. Romero."

"What lovely flowers," her mother said. "You should put them in a vase."

Elsa moved toward the kitchen to get a vase, but her father said: "Let your mother do it. Have a good time."

They left the house, and Bruce went around the car with her to open the door on the passenger side. Before he closed it, he made sure that she was seated.

"We're going to X2O," he said as they headed south on Broadway.

She had heard of the restaurant. It was on the old pier at the Yonkers waterfront. It was owned by the city's top chef. It was where the rich and the famous went, so she had never dreamed of going there.

The restaurant had valet parking, and after Bruce had stopped the car he came around and opened her door. It made her feel like a real lady.

Their table was in an intimate room, with low lights and a view of the river. The prices on the menu shocked her, and some of the items were a mystery. She decided to order the salmon because she knew what it was. Bruce ordered the scallops, and they shared a Caesar salad. He ordered a bottle of white wine, which the waiter opened and poured for him to taste. He raised his glass, took a sip, and nodded to the waiter that it was fine.

Her parents didn't drink wine, so she hadn't been exposed to it. Besides, she was under the legal age for drinking, which made her hesitate to drink the wine that the waiter had poured for her. He must have thought she was older than she was.

"Go ahead, try it," Bruce said. "It'll go with your fish."

She sipped the wine cautiously. She liked it, but she didn't want to drink too much of it.

Bruce asked her questions about the members of her family as if he was really interested in them: her father, her mother, her brother, and her grandmother. He also asked her about the family business, and he seemed impressed by the empire of supermarkets that her father and her uncle had built. He told her that someday he would like to have his own business, but in the meantime he had to gain some experience.

The dinner went fast even though they lingered over a dessert that was like nothing she ever had before, and when he stopped his car in front of her house he didn't get out right away. He leaned over and kissed her.

It wasn't her first kiss with a boy, but it was the first kiss that mattered. She tumbled into it, body and soul.

Before they said goodnight at her front door he said: "We're having a party tomorrow at our place. Would you like to come?"

"Sure," she said without hesitation.

The next day he picked her up at three in the afternoon and drove her to the house on Warburton where he lived with Larry and two other guys. It was a two-family house, and they had the lower half of it, which gave them access to the backyard.

There were about twenty people at the party, but no one else she had seen before except Larry. About half of them were girls, and after talking with some of them she learned that they were students at the college.

One of them, in clothes that didn't look warm enough for the time of year, was dancing by herself on the patio to rock music. Outside, there was a keg of beer, but except for the guys who went out to fill pitchers from it, most people stayed inside, drinking and talking in the living room. She would have liked to drink beer, which she was used to, but Bruce gave her a glass of something that he said she would love. It did taste good, and she didn't detect any alcohol in it, so she had another, and then another.

She couldn't remember how it happened, but the next thing she knew she was in a bedroom with the door closed, lying on a bed, and Bruce was taking down her pants. She tried to resist, but her arms and legs felt like rubber, and then he crouched over her, spreading her legs.

She felt a sharp pain, and then she felt him thrusting until with a shudder he finally stopped.

"Did you like that?" he asked.

"What?" she said, and she passed out.

After she regained her senses she didn't remember what had happened until she went to the bathroom and saw the blood in her panties. She was sure he wouldn't have raped her, so she must have consented under the influence of alcohol.

"Did you have a good time?" he asked her at the front door of her house.

"Yeah, sure. It was a great party."

He kissed her goodnight and said: "I love you."

"I love you too," she said in a daze.

She was glad that her parents were asleep so she didn't have to face their questions. It took her a while to get to sleep, but she finally did, and when she woke up the next morning the most important thing she remembered was his saying he loved her.

She had a morning class that ended at 11:25. It wasn't the class that she took with Gleny, so they didn't go to the cafeteria together. She went by herself, and going to a table with a sandwich on a tray she saw Bruce at a table with some friends.

But when she approached him smiling with joy he looked at her strangely.

"Do you know that girl?" a guy asked him.

"No, I don't know her," Bruce said. "I never saw her before."

As she staggered away from them she heard them laughing as if the whole thing had been a prank, with her as the victim.

Elsa turned into the driveway and parked her car alongside her father's car. She went into the house and found her mother in the kitchen, preparing dinner.

"How was your day?" her mother asked.

"It was fine," she said, opening the refrigerator to get a beer. "How was yours?"

"It was very busy. I had a long meeting with our banker. He thinks we should invest our excess cash."

"You have excess cash?" She found the opener in its usual place in a drawer where they also kept cellophane wrap and aluminum foil.

"We have more than we need for daily operations. But I like to have excess cash available, just in case we need it. I don't want it tied up in investments."

She opened the beer and took a sip. "I understand."

Her mother started putting pieces of chicken into a cast-iron skillet that was on the stove, over a flame. "Have you heard from Karl?"

"Karl?" She was surprised by the question. "Yeah, he's fine."

"He seemed like a nice young man."

"Well, don't get any ideas. He's married."

"He is? Oh. I wouldn't have guessed that he was married."

"You wouldn't have? Why not?"

"He didn't have a wedding ring. And also there was something about him. I mean, I had the feeling he was lonely."

"He *was* lonely. He missed his wife."

"That must have been it."

She had managed to avoid lying to her mother, at least directly. She had left out things that would have made her mother worry, and she could justify doing this, as she had justified leaving out things about Bruce that would have made her mother worry. In both situations telling her mother the whole truth would have alleviated her own anxiety, but she felt that the cost to her mother would have outweighed the benefit to her.

"How can I help you?" she asked her mother.

"You could watch the chicken while I wash the lettuce."

She was standing at the stove, turning a thigh in the skillet, when the phone rang. They had a phone in the kitchen, mounted on the wall, so she only had to take a few steps to read the caller ID, which said: "Out of area."

She let it ring, assuming it was yet another robocall. It couldn't have been Karl, who didn't know her home number and would have called her cell phone, so she didn't answer it. After ringing five times, it stopped, and whoever was calling didn't leave a message.

"Who was it?" her mother asked.

"A robot," she said. "They're really annoying."

"Yeah, they are. We keep getting them even though we're on a no-call list."

"That doesn't stop them." For some reason she was more annoyed than usual by this call, and after a moment she realized why. It could have been the guy who had threatened Karl. Somehow, he could have found her, and he could have called to threaten her and her family.

But how could he have found her? And if he had called to deliver a threat, why hadn't he left a message? She decided that it had only been another robocall, though she couldn't completely extinguish the other possibility.

She thought of calling Karl to see if he had gotten a call from the guy, but she decided that he couldn't have. He had taken the battery out of his cell phone, and there was no way the guy could have gotten the number of the guesthouse. So she didn't call Karl because she didn't want to make him worry.

That night she lay awake thinking about Bruce and worrying about Karl, with these two mental states encroaching on each other as if there was a connection between them. Of course there wasn't any connection. They were different situations, and they had nothing to do with each other.

But maybe they did. Maybe her helping Karl wasn't a pure act of charity. Maybe it was the last phase of a healing process in which she had to demonstrate that she could love an enemy, and even love a guy like the one who had hurt her.

TEN

THAT NIGHT KARL had trouble sleeping. He kept thinking about what the nun had told him about her own loss, and the point she had made about the relative value of jobs and human lives. He could now see that he had valued his job more than his wife and children. Of course, he should have known that their lives had more value than his job, but he was blinded by his feeling of injustice. His hatred of the people responsible for his job loss became stronger than his love for his family, and the group of people responsible expanded from the men who played financial games with the company to include people like the women who were now helping him. Yet at the time when he joined the white nationalist movement he saw it as his salvation.

It had started in the bar, where one night after work he met a guy from out of town. The guy was short, but he projected power with his compelling eyes and his mesmerizing voice. His name was Martin, and he was from western Pennsylvania. His father was a steel worker before they closed the mills in Pittsburgh, and though he never worked in a factory, he understood what it was like to work in a factory and lose your job.

"I'm here in Freiburg," he told Karl and the guys who had gathered around him, "because I know what happened here. I know what they did to your company. And you're not the only guys who have lost their jobs. There are millions of guys who have lost their jobs because of globalization and immigration."

"I understand why you blame globalization," Karl said. "But what does immigration have to do with it? We didn't lose our jobs to immigrants. We lost them to Mexico."

"Well, let me explain. When your ancestors came to this country, immigrants were white. But now they're not white, they're black and brown and yellow. And they're taking over the country.

They put a black man in the White House who wasn't even born in this country. You knew that, didn't you?"

"I thought he was born in Hawaii."

"He was born in Kenya, and they faked his papers so they could claim he was born here. And you know why they put a black man in the White House? So they can let in millions of nonwhite immigrants and turn us into a nonwhite country."

"Are you saying that whites would become a minority?"

"We're already becoming a minority, and when they take over, you know what will happen to us?"

"What will happen to us?"

"We'll become their slaves. We'll be picking cotton and hoeing tobacco."

"No, we won't. They have machines to do that kind of work."

"That was only a metaphor," Martin said, using a word that impressed them. "I meant we'll be doing the low-level work."

"But that's the kind of work that immigrants are doing now, isn't it?"

"You're right, but after they take over, immigrants won't be doing that kind of work. They'll be on welfare at our expense."

"I heard that most of them are on welfare now," a guy said.

"Most of them are," Martin said, "but after they take over, all of them will be on welfare."

"I have a question," Karl said. "Who exactly will take over? Immigrants?"

"No. They won't have the power. The coastal elites will have the power. They'll only use immigrants to make us a minority."

"How will they use them?"

"By getting them to vote for their candidates, just as they got them to vote for that black man in the White House."

"I heard on Fox News that he's a Muslim," a big guy said. "Is that true?"

"Of course it's true. Everything you hear on Fox News is true. But everything you hear on the liberal channels isn't true. It's fake news."

"So how do Muslins fit into what they're doing?"

"They're using Muslims to undermine Christians. You know, at one time Muslims almost dominated the world. They were driven out of Europe by Christians, but they're going back there through immigration, and they're coming here through immigration. That will lead to a situation where whites are a minority and Christians are a minority."

"You really think that's happening?" Karl asked, not quite ready to believe it.

"No, I don't think it's happening," Martin said, "I *know* it's happening. I have all the facts, and you can read them in a book I wrote."

"You wrote a book?"

"Yeah, I wrote a book, which a lot of people are reading now."

"Well, what can we do about what's happening?"

"We can organize, and we can fight the coastal elites. We can elect a president who will serve the people, not the elites. We can make America white again."

"Do you have a political party?"

"We have something better than a political party. We have a movement."

"What's it called?"

"It's called Patriots for a White America."

With nothing to do and nothing to live for, Karl joined the movement, which filled the void in his life and made him feel like he was someone.

Martin soon identified a candidate for president whom the movement could whole-heartedly support. He was a real estate developer from New York, who years ago had questioned the legitimacy of the black man in the White House. Despite criticism from the liberal media, he had stuck to his guns, and he had gained national attention for standing up to the coastal elites. He had come out strongly against globalization and immigration, promising to reverse them, to undo the damage they had done, and to make America great again, which everyone understood as meaning make America white again. What made him especially appealing to Karl was that he promised to bring back the jobs that had gone to other countries.

Their candidate began the campaign as an underdog, which helped members of the movement to relate with him, even though he was from a city they had only seen on television and he had grown up in a rich family. They watched with glee as he dismantled the other candidates in the debates, attacking their weaknesses and promoting his strengths. Under Martin's leadership, they worked for their candidate in the Ohio primary, organizing rallies, attending meetings, and handing out materials. At one meeting, which was in a school gym, Martin was explaining why people should vote for their candidate and making the argument that he would make America white again.

A woman, who looked like a school teacher, raised her hand and said: "What you're saying sounds racist. Is this guy a racist?"

"Now, that's a word that the liberal media use to make us ashamed of being white. Are you ashamed of being white?"

"No, but—"

"I'm glad you're not ashamed of being white. You shouldn't be. You should be proud of being white. It was white people who founded this country and made it great. And if it's all right to have black pride, why isn't it all right to have white pride?"

The woman had no answer.

"What about jobs?" a man in back asked. "He says he's going to bring back the jobs that went to other countries. How's he going to do that?"

"He's going to stop imports from those countries. Everything we import from China now we used to make here, so we'll make those products here, and that'll bring back the jobs."

"What about immigrants?" another man asked. "How's he going to stop all those Mexicans from coming into our country and taking our jobs?"

"He's going to build a wall on the Mexican border."

"Will that stop them from coming in?"

"It sure as hell will. It'll be the highest wall that was ever built."

"What about the illegal immigrants who are already here?"

"He's going to deport them."

"But some of them have children who were born here," a woman in front pointed out.

"That's their problem. They shouldn't have come here and had children."

"What about the immigrants from other countries?"

"He's going to make it harder, if not impossible, for them to get visas. That'll stop all the Muslims who are coming here."

The crowd really liked what they heard, and in future rallies supporters of their candidate could be heard chanting: "Build the wall, build the wall."

In the primary on March 15 a number of counties in the south of Ohio, which bordered Kentucky, and counties in the east, where there were coal mines—their candidate promised to revive coal mining—were won by their candidate. But most of the other counties were won by the current governor, so he captured the state's sixty-six delegates. Surrounded by counties won by the governor, the county that contained Freiburg was won by their candidate, and Karl was proud of this accomplishment. Though their candidate didn't win in Ohio, he won the other primaries that were held that day in Florida, Illinois, Missouri, and North Carolina, and with his triumph three weeks earlier in the Pennsylvania primary, he took a commanding lead in the number of delegates pledged to him.

By early May their candidate was the presumptive nominee for the Republican Party, and on June 19 he became the official nominee. From then on, Martin asked Karl and the other guys in Freiburg who had joined the movement to concentrate their efforts on winning Ohio, a key state, while Martin concentrated his efforts on winning Pennsylvania, another key state. If their candidate could win those states, he could win the election.

Karl was still nominally living in a room at his cousin's house, but he was rarely there because he was so often traveling and attending rallies for their candidate. They didn't go to the big cities, where there were a lot of nonwhites who were certain to vote for the Democrat. Instead, they focused on the towns and rural areas, where people were receptive to their messages about globalization and immigration. There were other towns like Freiburg where factories had closed and the jobs had gone to other countries. The people at the rallies liked hearing that their candidate would bring back jobs, deport immigrants, and build a wall on the Mexican border. Those were the main selling points.

Unfortunately, in early October the liberal media released a video in which their candidate boasted that he could grab women by the pussy and get away with it because he was a star. With this revelation only a month before the election, there was cause for alarm because the white women who supported their candidate would be offended.

The next evening Karl got a phone call from Linda, who called him periodically to see how he was doing. He assumed it was only a routine call, but after their preliminary exchange she asked: "Did you see that video of your candidate?"

"Yeah, I saw it," he said, "but it's a fake."

"How could it be a fake? It was released by reputable media, and that was his voice on the video. I recognized it."

"They can do things with voices. They have the technology."

"Who do you mean?"

"The people who want to stop our candidate."

"I think you've been watching Fox News too much."

"I didn't get it from Fox News, I got it from Martin, who knows what's happening."

"The way you talk about this guy," Linda said, "it sounds like he's got you under his power."

"He hasn't got me under his power. But I respect him. I mean, he's our leader."

"If he's your leader, then he's leading you astray. You're supporting a man who exploits women and treats them like objects."

"If that's what he does, I won't support him, but I don't believe that's what he does. He promotes women in his organization, and he has women involved in his campaign. So why should I believe that video?"

"Because it's true. It reveals him for what he is."

"Well, you're being led astray by the liberal media."

"Karl," she said, "you've been brainwashed by Martin. You believe whatever this guy says. And I'm telling you, it'll get you into trouble."

"I don't see how. He's been right about everything, and he's still predicting that our candidate will win the election."

"Maybe he will, but he won't win Minnesota. And if he wins the election, it'll be the worst thing that ever happened to our country."

Their candidate did win the election, thanks to his victories in Ohio and Pennsylvania. Karl believed that their movement had helped him to win those states, and he would have rested on this accomplishment if Martin hadn't contacted him and told him that the coastal elites were working to undo the election.

Before their candidate could assume office the government's intelligence agencies concluded that Russia had interfered with the election. Their review had been ordered by the black man while he was still in the White House, and it was designed to undermine the legitimacy of their candidate's victory. Meanwhile, the coastal elites were organizing demonstrations to oppose the policies for which their candidate had been elected, and the liberal media were covering these events, which made it seem like most people were against these policies. The issue that attracted the strongest opposition was immigration, especially in cities that were self-designated as sanctuaries for illegal immigrants.

As he watched these events unfold on television Karl felt that the enemies of the people were trying to remove the president from office, and he was frustrated because he didn't know what he could do to stop them. His feelings intensified to a point where he hated them for trying to undo the only good thing he had done since he lost his job.

In the early spring Martin began to implement a plan to stop the enemies of the people. It was to send representatives of the movement to key cities where people were protesting against the president, and to demonstrate support for him. Invited to participate in these demonstrations, Karl jumped at the opportunity. So he spent the next few months traveling with the movement through the Midwest, pursuing their mission. They were in Altoona when Martin decided they should go and demonstrate at a protest in New York City that was being sponsored by a number of pro-immigration groups. The purpose of being there was to show the country that people who had elected the president supported his policies on immigration and that people who opposed his policies were un-American.

With about a dozen members of the movement, Karl traveled by bus from Altoona to Philadelphia, where a former school bus painted olive drab met them and drove them to a farm in New Jersey. There, under Martin's leadership, the members of several white nationalist movements were gathering for the demonstration. Though these movements differed in some respects, they were all committed to the mission of making America white again.

Before they embarked for the demonstration, in a fleet of former school buses all painted olive drab and with no markings, Martin gave them a pep talk, saying: "We're going into enemy territory. This city is filled with screaming liberals, and they can get violent, so watch out. Remember, they hate us, and if they could get away with it, they'd lock us up."

"If they attack us," one guy said, "can we fight back?"

"Just hold your ground. If we hurt them, it'll be used against us." Looking at a huddle of guys with swastika bands on their arms, Martin told them: "Take off those armbands. It'll only give them ammunition. There're more Jews in this city than you can shake a stick at."

"I don't want to shake a stick at them," one of the neo-Nazis said. "I want to get rid of them."

"Jews will not replace us," the members of his group chanted. "Jews will not replace us."

"Okay, okay," Martin said. "Now, Karl and Wayne and Ethan and Mac, I want you guys in the front row. You're going to deliver our message to them."

The buses took them to a highway that ran through rural land

and then through suburbs and then through a tunnel under the Hudson River and out into the daylight, where they encountered traffic. From then on they moved slowly, stopped by traffic lights and traffic jams, but they finally arrived at their point of disembarkment. As they walked from there to the place where the demonstration was being held, following Martin, they gaped like tourists at the buildings that towered over the street.

The crowd was thickening, and they had to push their way through it to reach their destination at the corner of a side street and an avenue. Martin told them where to stand, positioning Karl and the three other selected guys in the front row. Across the street were demonstrators from the other side, holding signs with messages that opposed the movement. Directly across from him was a brown girl with a sign that said LOVE WILL PREVAIL. If she hadn't been brown, she would have been pretty. And she didn't look at him as if she hated him, she looked at him as if she loved him. But when he saw the cross hanging from a cord around her neck, he knew what kind of love it was, and he dismissed it, believing it was fake.

Then suddenly there was a shot, and a gun came over his head and landed on the pavement in front of him. Whatever impulse made him pick up the gun, he was conscious of the girl across the street as he stooped and did what felt like the right thing, though he regretted his action when the cops grabbed him.

As they hauled him away in the back seat of their car, he knew he had a witness who could testify that he hadn't fired the gun, but he couldn't count on her to go to the police and tell them what she had seen, and he had no way of finding her. He could only hope there was a video from a surveillance camera that showed he hadn't fired the gun.

After making him wait for a long time in an interview room, a tough-looking detective came in and sat down at the table opposite him and asked: "Why did you do it?"

"I didn't do it," he insisted.

"Oh, come on. We know you did it. We caught you with the weapon in your hand, and yours were the only fingerprints on it."

"But I didn't fire it."

"Then what was it doing in your hand?"

"It came over my head and landed on the pavement in front of me, and I picked it up."

The detective looked skeptical. "Why would you have picked up that gun?"

"I don't know. I guess so no one else could use it."

"You expect me to believe that a guy in a group promoting hatred would act out of concern for people?"

"I almost don't believe it myself, it was such a stupid thing to do. But that's why I picked up the gun, and I have a witness."

"You mean a guy in your group?"

"No. I mean a girl who was standing across the street from me, demonstrating on the other side. She saw what happened."

"Good luck in finding her. The crowd has scattered, and if she was on the other side, why would she testify on your behalf?"

"I don't know. I just have a feeling she would."

"Well, you can sit here and think about it. If you confess, you could get out of prison in ten years with good behavior. But if you don't confess, you could be there for life."

By the time he awoke the next morning he had decided to break with the movement. They hadn't saved him, they had led him astray. And when he was arrested, none of the guys who were standing with him—Wayne or Ethan or Mac—came forward and testified on his behalf. They knew he hadn't fired the shot, but they had done nothing to help him. The only people who had helped him were the girl across the street and the nun at this college campus. They were the ones who had saved him.

He got out of bed and went into the kitchen and made coffee, using the percolator and the Santo Domingo coffee that Elsa had provided. It was still too early to call her, so he took his mug of coffee into the living room and sat down on the sofa. As he held the warm mug, which was white with something written on it in small blue letters, he recognized the prayer he had learned in elementary school: "Make me an instrument of your peace. Where there is hatred, let me sow love…" And reading the rest of it, he felt as if Elsa was saying it, praying that he would learn from what had happened and move on with his life.

Around eight he called her cell phone, and she answered after one ring as if she was waiting to hear from someone.

"It's Karl," he said. "Could you come over here this morning?"

"Yeah, sure. I don't have a class." She paused and then asked: "Are you all right?"

"Yeah, I'm all right. There's something I want to tell you."

"I'll be there in about twenty minutes. Okay?"

"Okay." He hung up the phone and went back to the kitchen, where he got a piece of bread and toasted it, not so much because he was hungry as because he needed to do something to kill time while he waited for her.

When he heard a knock on the door he went and opened it without asking who it was, and seeing her, he stepped aside and let her in, saying: "Thanks for coming."

"No problem," she said. "I'm free on Wednesdays."

"Would you like some coffee?"

"No, thanks. I already had some."

"Well, have a seat," he said, indicating a chair near the sofa.

She sat down in the chair, and he sat down on the sofa so that they were facing each other. She waited for him to begin the conversation.

"I decided to break with the movement," he told her.

"You did?" She smiled. *"Gracias a Dios."*

"I realized that it's not who I am, or at least it's not who I want to be. In fact, I think your sign at the demonstration had the right message."

She nodded, looking happy for him.

"Without your help," he told her, "I never would have found a way to free myself from their influence, so I want to thank you."

"You don't have to thank me. I only gave you a safe haven."

"You helped me see that I was on the wrong side."

"There's no wrong side or right side. There's only one side, where we can come together."

"Wherever that is, I'm there with you. And the first thing I have to do is tell the police who I think killed that girl."

"Okay. And if you tell them what you know, then you might not have to stay in the area."

"I might have to stay and identify the guy," he said. "I mean, if they catch him."

"If they don't catch him, he can still threaten you."

"Yeah, I know. He can also still threaten you and your family. That's a big reason why I want to help the police catch him."

"But what about *your* family?"

"He doesn't know about my family. I didn't share my personal information with those guys. But he could know about you."

"How? You think he saw me follow you to the police station?"

"He could have, though he probably didn't. He probably snuck off after firing the shot."

"Then how did he know you talked with the police?"

"He must have learned that from the guys who were with me. They stood there and watched me being hauled away."

She was silent for a while, thinking. "Well, let's assume that he didn't see me follow you to the police station. And let's assume that he was threatening anyone who helped you but no one in particular. Then I'm not in danger."

"You're in danger if he finds you with me."

"Well, he won't find you, so he won't find me."

"As long as he's on the loose he could find me, and he could find you with me, so I have to help the police catch him."

"If you go to the police today, I can go with you."

"That's what I was hoping," he said. "I have no idea how to get to that precinct."

"I know how to get there. We take the train and then a subway. It's only a few blocks from the subway station."

"Then I'll call Detective Ferraro and make an appointment. Can you go any time today?"

"Yeah, I can go any time."

He found the number on the paper where he had written it, and he called it.

A woman answered, asked who was calling, and put him through to the detective.

"Thanks for calling," the detective said. "What's on your mind?"

"I have some information for you. I should have given to you before, and I'm sorry I didn't, but I want to give it to you now. Can we meet today?"

"Yeah, we can. How about eleven thirty?"

"That's fine. I'll see you then."

Elsa found a train schedule in her pocketbook and determined that there was an express that left Yonkers at 10:00 and arrived at Grand Central at 10:29, which would give them more than enough time to get to the precinct. If they took a later train, it would be tight, and he didn't want to be late for his appointment.

It was only a little after nine now, so they had time before they had to leave for the Yonkers station, and Elsa suggested that they go and tell Sister Solana about his decision. He agreed, and they left the guesthouse, locking the door, and headed for the convent. On the way she texted Sister Solana, who was coming out to meet them when they arrived.

"Let's go into the cloister," she said. "We can talk there."

She let them through a gate and into an enclosed area with a colonnade on three sides and an open side that faced the river. There were small trees and benches in the center. They sat down on one of the benches, with Karl in the middle, Elsa on his left and Sister Solana on his right. He felt comfortable between them.

"So what's happening?" Sister Solana said.

"I made a decision," Karl told her. "I'm going to break with the movement, and I'm going to tell the police who I think killed the girl."

"I'm glad for you." She put a hand gently on his shoulder.

"I have an appointment with the detective at eleven thirty this morning, and with the information I'm going to give him, I hope they can catch that guy."

"Until they catch him," Elsa pointed out, "Karl will still be in danger, so he can't go back to his wife."

"I understand. So you decided to go back to your wife?"

"Yeah, I did. If she'll take me back."

"From what you told me, I think she'll take you back. I think she'll forgive you."

"I hope she will. If I was her, I don't know if I would. I mean, after the way I treated her."

"You didn't value her the way you should have," the sister told him, "but you didn't reject her. You only had a meltdown."

"We all have meltdowns," Elsa said.

"You had a meltdown?"

"Oh, yeah, I did. I completely lost it, and if it wasn't for Sister Solana, I wouldn't be sitting here with you now."

"None of us can make it through this world without help from others," the sister said. "So when you get yourself together, you can help someone."

"I don't know where to start."

"Start with your wife and your children. If you can be a good husband and a good father, that'll go a long way."

"But I have to find a job."

"You'll find a job in St. Paul. Their economy is booming."

By now he no longer doubted the sister's knowledge of this subject. "You think I'll have a better chance of finding a job in St. Paul than I had in Freiburg?"

"I know you will. Your wife found a job there."

"But she went back to college, and she learned new skills."

"Well, you can learn new skills in a training program."

"How would I pay for it?"

"I'm sure they have financial assistance programs in that state. They have an advanced healthcare program."

"But it'll be hard to leave Freiburg. My family's lived there for seven generations."

"My family lived in the Dominican Republic for more than thirty generations," the sister said. "I mean, if you count my Taino ancestors. But my father left his home country, and he came here. So if immigrants can leave their home countries, you can leave Freiburg and go to St. Paul."

"I guess I can. So I'd be an immigrant."

"You'd be a migrant. And the people in Minnesota might not welcome you," the sister said with a playful smile, "because you're from Ohio."

"And you're a Reds fan," Elsa said.

He laughed. "Yeah. Are they mostly Scandinavian there?"

"In St. Paul they're mostly German and Irish, but there are also African Americans, Asians, and Latinos, including some Dominicans. The city's not all white."

"Well, that's a lot different from Freiburg."

"It's more representative of our country, so it's a good place to make a new start."

They were silent for a while, and then he said: "As soon as I'm done with the detective, I'm going to call my wife, and I'm going to ask her if she'll take me back."

"I believe she will, but just to make sure, I'll pray that she will."

"Thank you, sister," Karl said, putting an arm around her. "Thanks for everything."

ELEVEN

INSTEAD OF DRIVING her car to the Yonkers station, where she might have trouble finding a parking space, she called a taxi, which arrived within five minutes. It was the grumpy driver, who for some reason was a Red Sox fan, and he was a little less grumpy this season because his team was doing well. She got along fine with him, knowing enough about baseball to talk with him about it. He left them in front of the station, where several taxis were waiting. They were all Crown Victorias, with no markings except the license plates to identify them as taxis, but everyone who took taxis knew who they were.

They went into the station, which had been designed and constructed in another era, and it had recently been restored, no doubt because of the new apartment buildings that were going up along the waterfront. She got two round-trip tickets from the machine and led Karl up the stairs to the platform, where people were waiting for trains running south. Their train was on time, and she found seats on the side that faced the river. She let him have the seat at the window so he could enjoy the splendid view. With people around them, they couldn't talk about what was on their minds, so as soon as the conductor had punched their tickets she leaned her head back on the seat and closed her eyes.

She hated Bruce for what he had done to her, and she hated herself for letting him do it. She avoided the campus because she was afraid she would run into Bruce, who would make her feel even more worthless for letting herself be used in a game to prove her inferiority, and also because she was afraid she would run into Gleny, who would make her feel even more stupid for believing that Bruce cared about her.

On top of her feelings of worthlessness and stupidity was her worry that she could be pregnant. She was in the middle of her monthly cycle when she was most likely to conceive. Recalling what had happened to Gleny's cousin, she cringed at the thought that the same thing could happen to her. She couldn't imagine facing her parents and telling them she was pregnant, especially her father. It would break his heart. It would be better for her to get killed in an accident, maybe by walking in front of a bus. But she couldn't do that to a bus driver. It would be better to kill herself, maybe by jumping off the cliff into the river. But what if they found out in an autopsy that she was pregnant? It would be better to abort the baby. But that would condemn her to eternal damnation. She was finally reconciled to having the baby, though she prayed every hour of every day that she wasn't pregnant.

During this time she was cutting her classes, and to hide from her parents what she was doing she left the house at the usual times and got on the bus that ran in a loop, going north on Palisade Avenue and Broadway, then east on Executive Boulevard, then south on Nepperhan Avenue, then west on Walsh Road, south on Palisade, west on Prospect Street, north on Riverdale Avenue, and finally west on Larkin Plaza to the station. At the last stop she had to get off, but she was first in line for the next bus, and she would ride the loop until it was time for her to go home. She got to know the bus drivers, who must have wondered about her. On one trip the big black driver kindly asked her if she was all right. She told him she was fine, and after that she avoided riding on his bus. If he was the driver, she killed time in the little park next to the station, where there was a statue of Ella Fitzgerald, and she got on the next bus.

She was still sinking, drowning in sorrow, when something happened to buoy her up. She had her period, so she could stop worrying about being pregnant. She thanked God, knowing that since it wouldn't be reflected in her body she could hide what had happened. She could keep it to herself. She would never have to tell anyone about it.

But her relief was temporary. Not being pregnant didn't take away the humiliation that Bruce had inflicted on her. It didn't stop her from hating him, from hating herself.

After the first time she cut the class that she took with Gleny, her friend texted her, asking her if she was all right. She didn't respond, and Gleny continued texting her until she responded, saying she was sick. For a while this lie kept Gleny away, but then her friend asked if she could come and see her. She didn't want Gleny to come to her house because it might reveal to her parents that she was cutting classes, so she agreed to meet Gleny at the pizza place on Palisade Avenue.

When she arrived at the pizza place Gleny was sitting in a booth with a soda, and seeing her, Gleny said: *"Dios mío. Qué te pasó?"*

"What do you mean?" Elsa asked, sliding into the booth.

"You look half dead. Did you have that horrible flu?"

"No. I just haven't been feeling well."

Gleny looked at her doubtfully. "Did something happen with that guy?"

"You mean Bruce? No, nothing happened."

"Did you go out with him?"

"Yeah, I did. He took me to a restaurant on the waterfront."

"The one where the rich and famous people go?"

She nodded. "Yeah. It was no big deal."

"And that was all?"

"Yeah, that was all."

Looking puzzled, Gleny said: "If you didn't have that flu, and if nothing happened with that guy, then why do you look half dead?"

"I don't know. I guess I'm depressed." She knew her friend would understand because they had taken a psychology course that covered depression. "It could be my hormones."

"It could be. Have you seen a doctor?"

"No, I haven't. I don't want my parents to know about it."

"Why don't you want your parents to know about it?"

"I don't want to disappoint them."

"If you're depressed because of your hormones, it's not your fault. We learned that depression is an illness, right?"

"I know we did. But I still feel like it's my fault."

After a long silence Gleny said: "I think there's something you're not telling me. And if there is, I wish you'd open up."

"You'll make me feel even more stupid," she said, finally unable to hold back the tears.

"No, I won't," Gleny said. "I'm your friend."

"Well, you were right about that guy."

"What do you mean?"

"He only wanted one thing from me, and he got it."

"What? You had sex with him?"

"I didn't know what I was doing. He gave me a drink that didn't taste like it had alcohol in it, but it did, and I was stupid enough to drink it. I not only drank it, I drank another, and the next thing I knew—" She was sobbing now.

Gleny reached across the table and took her hand, saying: "*Lo siento tanto.*"

It took her a while to realize that Gleny was crying along with her, and that made her open up completely. "The next day I saw him in the cafeteria with his friends. I was glad to see him, but when I approached him one of them asked him if he knew me, and he said didn't know me, he said he never saw me before."

"At least that was true. He never saw *you*, he only saw an object."

"Well, that's what he made me feel like. He made me feel like a piece of shit."

"I understand," Gleny said. "But you can't let that asshole ruin your life."

"He already has ruined my life. I can't face my parents."

"You're eating meals with them, aren't you?"

"Yeah, but I'm not really facing them. I'm pretending that everything's all right, and I can't stand lying to them."

"Then tell them the truth."

"I can't," she said. "I don't want to disappoint them."

"I know you don't, but if you keep cutting classes, sooner or later they'll find out."

"By then I might not be around."

"*Madre de Dios.* You mustn't even think about that. You have everything to live for."

"I have nothing to live for."

"Your parents love you," Gleny said, taking both of her hands. "I love you. A lot of people love you. So you have reasons to love yourself."

"But how can I ever love myself after what I did?"

"You can start by forgiving yourself. I know it's hard, but you can do it. And maybe someday you can even forgive that asshole."

This conversation helped her, but it didn't restore her self-worth. She attended her last classes before the spring break, she told her professors she had been sick, and she promised to make up the work she had missed. But her heart wasn't in it, and though she spent time during the break doing makeup assignments, she didn't do her best work. She didn't see any point in getting good grades, except to make her parents happy, so she only did what was necessary. She didn't tell her parents about her absences, and she didn't tell them what Bruce had done to her. But she didn't succeed in hiding from them that something was wrong, and one evening while she was helping with the dishes her mother asked her if she was all right.

"Yeah, I'm fine," she said, taking a plate from her mother.

"You don't seem to have a lot of spirit."

"Do I usually have a lot of spirit?"

"Yes. But lately you've been acting depressed."

"Well, I *am* depressed. I don't know why, but that's how I feel."

"Is it because you don't have a boyfriend?"

"No, it's not. I don't need a boyfriend."

"You probably don't, but girls your age have them."

"They brag about having them, but they could just be making them up."

"They could be. Does Gleny have a boyfriend?"

"No, she doesn't. With all the science courses she's taking, she doesn't have time for one."

"Then you don't feel you should have one?"

"No. It's the last thing I need right now."

"So maybe it's your hormones," her mother said. "When I was your age, I went up and down like a roller coaster."

"You did?" She couldn't imagine her steady mother going up and down like a roller coaster.

"Oh, yeah. One day I was the happiest girl in the whole world, and the next day I was the saddest girl. And it had nothing to do with boys."

"What did it have to do with?"

"I never knew. But I grew out of it."

"Then maybe I'll grow out of it," she said, reaching for another plate to dry.

"You will," her mother said. "But if anything's wrong, I want you to tell me. I don't want you to keep it to yourself."

As she dried the plate she made a decision. "Well, there *is* something wrong. A few weeks ago I met a boy, and I fell in love with him."

Her mother waited for her to continue.

"He didn't love me back, and that hurt me."

"I understand. When people don't love you back, it hurts."

She hadn't told her mother the whole truth, but she had told her the basic truth, and it made her feel a little better. "So that's why I'm depressed."

"Well, you'll get over it. Just remember," her mother said, "if that boy didn't love you back, it was *his* problem, not yours."

This conversation also helped her, but it didn't raise her self-worth to the level where it had been before. She did better at her courses, and she did everything else she was supposed to do, including her job at the checkout counter of the supermarket on Palisade Avenue, but often at night, as she lay in the dark silence of her room, she felt as if there was nothing to stop her from falling into an abyss.

She went to church every Sunday with her family, and she took communion even though she felt unworthy of it because she had committed a mortal sin, but if she hadn't joined her family in this sacrament her mother would have known she hadn't told her the whole truth, so she went along with it, feeling like an imposter.

One afternoon in late April she was sitting on a bench by the path that overlooked the river. It was a spot where she could get away from everyone and be alone with her feelings. She was gazing at the rippled water, yearning to disappear under the surface, when someone stopped in front of her and asked: "Are you all right?"

It was a woman, younger than her mother, with brown skin, dark hair, and dark eyes that were brimming with compassion. The wooden cross hanging outside her top identified her as a nun. "Yeah, I'm fine."

"You don't look fine," the nun said. "Do you mind if I sit down with you?"

She did mind. She didn't like having any intrusion on her solitude. But if this woman was a nun she couldn't be rude to her, so she said: "No, I don't mind."

"I'm Sister Solana," the woman said, extending her hand.

Elsa took it and limply shook it. "I'm Elsa."

"I assume you're a student."

"Yeah, I am."

"You haven't taken a course with me."

"No. I haven't."

"What year are you?"

"I'm a sophomore."

"Do you have a major?"

"Yeah, I do. I'm majoring in psychology."

The sister nodded as if this was good. "From the way you were gazing at the river, I got the feeling that you're unhappy."

"I am," she said, unable to hold back her feelings. There was something about this woman that made her want to open up and tell her everything.

Leaning back in the bench and looking at the river, the sister said: "Tell me about it."

She poured out her heart to the sister, telling her how she fell in love and how the guy led her on, and how he took the only thing he wanted from her, and how he discarded her as if he no longer had any use for her.

The sister listened to her without interrupting. She was silent for a while after hearing about the scene in the cafeteria, and then she asked: "How do you feel about this guy?"

"I *hate* him," Elsa said with passion. "I hate all guys, except for my father and my brother, and I especially hate white guys."

"You blame them for what this guy did to you?"

"Yeah, I do. When I see a white guy, I think of him, and I remember what he did to me."

"Besides hating him, how do you feel?"

"I feel worthless. I feel like I don't deserve to live."

"You blame yourself for what happened?"

"Yeah. I know it wasn't my fault, but I feel that somehow it was. Does that make sense?"

"It makes a lot of sense," the sister said. "It's what girls usually feel when something like that happens to them."

"But why do I feel this way?"

"I'll tell you why, but first tell me where your parents are from."

"They're from the Dominican Republic."

"Really? So are mine. Were you born here?"

"No, I was born there."

"So was I," the sister said. *"Así que ambas somos dominicanas."*

"Sí, las somos." She wondered if their coming from the same home country had made her open up to the sister.

"Did you tell your parents what happened to you?"

"No. I told my mother I fell in love with a boy who didn't love me back, but I didn't tell her the whole truth."

"What about your father?"

"Oh, no. I couldn't tell *him.*"

"Do you have any brothers or sisters?"

"I only have a younger brother."

"So you're the first child, and I bet you're the first in your family to go to college."

"I am, but what does that have to do with it?"

"You're the pride and joy of your parents, and whether or not they know what happened, you feel you've brought disgrace to them. It's embedded in our culture," the sister explained "That's why it's harder to face your father than your mother."

"Well, I *have* brought disgrace to them. I mean, I had sex before I was married. That's a mortal sin, isn't it?"

"According to church doctrine it is, but it happens, and it's not the end of the world."

"I feel like it's the end of the world."

"I understand, but it doesn't have to ruin your life." The sister paused. "How are you doing in your courses?"

"I'm not doing well. I cut classes for about two weeks, but after talking with a friend I went back and tried to catch up."

"Did you tell your friend what happened?"

"Yeah. For a while I didn't tell her because I thought she'd make me feel even more stupid. She warned me about that guy."

"So it helped to talk with your friend?"

"It did, but not enough. I still feel worthless."

"Well, you won't regain your self-worth by hating that guy, or by hating white guys. You'll regain it by love."

"I can't love after what happened."

"You love your parents, and you love your brother, and you love your friend, don't you?"

"Yeah, but that's easy."

The sister smiled. "That's what our Lord said. It's easy to love your family and friends. But it's hard to love your enemies."

"I can't ever love that guy."

"You don't have to, but you can love people beyond your family and your friend. If we love others, we know God."

"That sounds familiar."

"It's from a letter by St. John, but you need to understand the meaning of love in this sense. It's action, it's not a feeling. You have to do something for others."

She tried to understand. "But what can I do?"

"You know the church of San Pedro?"

"Yeah. I go there with my family. We don't live near there anymore, but they have a mass in Spanish that my grandmother can understand."

"Well, you can join our mission there. We have a food pantry, we have immigration services, we have English classes, and we have an after-school program. I think you'd be good in the after-school program."

"But I have classes, and I have a job at a supermarket."

"The one on Palisade Avenue?"

"Yeah. My father and my uncle own it."

"Really? I shop there. Do you work at the checkout counter?"

"Yeah, on Fridays and on weekends."

"That explains why I haven't seen you there. I only shop there during the week. Well, we can work around your classes and your job. The kids arrive from school between two-thirty and three. Their parents are working, so we take care of them and help them with their schoolwork."

"I think I could do that," Elsa said, encouraged by the sister's faith in her.

"When does your last class end tomorrow?"

"At two thirty-five."

"Then meet me in front of Main Hall after class. I'll take you there and get you started."

The next afternoon Sister Solana drove her to San Pedro and introduced her to the volunteers who were working that day. They included a nun who must have been her grandmother's age and a retired teacher, a white guy who she later learned had come from Cuba with his family at the age of six.

Sister Solana led her into the large room where the kids were gathered. They were sitting at tables in groups according to their school level. The sister asked her to join a volunteer at a table with three kids in the first grade. The woman's name was Clarita, and from her accent she sounded Puerto Rican. She was around thirty.

Clarita introduced the kids to Elsa, and then she continued working with them. They all had books with pictures and words, and Clarita was helping them review what they had covered in class that day. The kids, two girls and a boy, were adorable.

Just by watching Clarita in action, Elsa know that Sister Solana had found the right thing for her, and she couldn't wait to have her own group of kids.

After the kids left to go home Clarita lingered at the table to exchange information with Elsa. It turned out that Clarita was a graduate of St. Catherine, with a master's in social work, and that she was serving the community of South Yonkers. She had a very busy schedule, but she still found time to volunteer at San Pedro two afternoons a week.

"I wasn't an immigrant," Clarita told her, "but I felt like one, and I had a lot of trouble at school until a wonderful teacher helped me. I'll always remember what she did for me, and I want to do that for these kids."

The next day Elsa was assigned to two kids, a girl and a boy. The girl was from El Salvador, and the boy was from Honduras. The girl seemed naturally happy, but the boy was sad. She had learned from Sister Solana that his father was stymied by obstacles to joining his family, and that the boy missed his father.

He had enormous brown eyes, which were filled with sorrow. It made Elsa feel lucky that she hadn't been separated from her parents. And her heart went out to all the kids who were separated from mothers and fathers by the heartless bureaucratic process of immigration.

By helping those kids she restored her self-worth at least to the level where she could take a compliment from Sister Adele, who worked with her in the after-school program. The nun told her: "You're really good at this, so keep doing it."

In the summer the kids didn't have school, so Elsa continued helping Sister Solana in her mission by teaching ESL to adults, who sometimes had to bring their kids with them if a grandmother wasn't available to babysit. She gave the kids paper and crayons, which kept them busy while she was teaching their mothers.

In the fall, after a long discussion with Sister Solana, she confirmed her major in psychology. She believed the degree would enable her to help people beyond schoolwork and language. She had learned from the adults in her ESL classes that they were undergoing tremendous stresses in their lives, and they didn't have healthcare coverage to pay for treatment. Her vision was to start a clinic at the church where people could get free therapy.

Sister Solana supported her in this effort, and even helped her raise money for it. For her master's thesis Sister Solana helped her to prepare a business plan for the project, which they launched a year later. It enabled her to apply what she had learned in college to help people who otherwise wouldn't get treatment.

During the years while she was working on her doctorate with Sister Solana as her dissertation mentor she always had the issue of immigration on her mind, and when they heard the Republican candidate for president attacking immigrants, calling them rapists and murderers, they prepared and disseminated information which showed that he was wrong, which proved that immigrants made enormous contributions to the country.

When Trump was elected president, they were shocked and dismayed, but they soon recovered and organized demonstrations against his injurious policies.

Their demonstration on the day when they faced the white nationalists near Trump Tower was triggered by a series of policies that would deprive immigrants of their rights, including those who had lived in the country for many years with the understanding that they were safe. It was hearing the cries of alarm and despair from women who had fled their home countries in real fear of being raped, tortured, and killed by gangs that roused Elsa to go with Sister Solana to that demonstration. And the shot that killed the Haitian girl seemed to validate her hatred of white guys, which over the years had never completely gone away.

She was alerted to her present surroundings by the train going underground at 96th Street. It would take them about ten more minutes to get to the station, but some restless people in the car were already stirring. Karl was sitting upright in his seat, looking alert and ready to fulfill the commitment he had made.

When the train finally stopped at Grand Central they got off and followed the throng of people up the stairs and into the concourse. They had almost an hour before the appointment, so Elsa asked: "Would you like a coffee?"

"Yeah. That would be good."

She led him out of the station and onto a side street, where after walking a half block they came to a small coffee shop. It wasn't a chain, it was a local place, and it was owned by one of her cousins.

"I see they have Santo Domingo coffee," he said. "Is this one of your father's businesses?"

"No, it's a cousin's." She went to the counter and ordered two coffees, which she carried to a high-top. "If you want cream, it's on the counter."

"Black is fine," he said. "Do all Dominicans have their own businesses?"

"A lot of them do. They're happy to work for other people, but they're happier if they work for themselves."

"I guess it gives them more control over their lives."

"Yeah. But there are risks in having your own business."

After paying the check she led Karl back into the station and toward the subway, down the escalator and through the turn style, using her card. From the way he stuck by her, she guessed that he had never been in a subway before. They went down the stairs to the platform and waited for a local train. When one stopped, they stepped aside to let the people get off, and then they got on. There were two empty seats near the door, so they occupied them.

As the train moved forward she noticed that almost all of the passengers were engrossed in their smartphones, completely unaware of their surroundings. The subway could have gone to the Bronx without stopping, and they wouldn't have noticed.

They stopped at 50th and at 59th and then as the train began to slow for the stop at 68th she got up and grabbed a vertical bar, with Karl following her. They got off at 68th and in a crowd of Hunter College students they climbed the stairs and emerged on the street. She got her bearings and headed toward the precinct.

"Are you all right?" she asked Karl as they walked along.

"Yeah, I'm fine. I'm a little nervous."

"I understand. Just tell him what you know."

At the entrance of the precinct they were checked by security, and then they were led to a waiting area. They were five minutes early, so she figured they wouldn't have to wait long, but it was almost noon when Karl was finally allowed to meet with Detective Ferraro.

As he got up from the chair next to her, Elsa reached for his hand and squeezed it, silently saying: *"Que Dios te ayude."*

She sat and waited, remembering the events from the time they faced each other across the street with opposing messages to the time they boarded the train in Yonkers for this meeting with the detective. It had been a long struggle to get Karl to the point where he was ready to break with the movement, to tell the police what he knew about the killing, and to go back to his family. She had played a minor role in the process, with Sister Solana playing the major role, but she had contributed to his redemption, and she felt that by helping him she had finally redeemed herself from hating Bruce, from hating white guys.

TWELVE

WHEN KARL ENTERED the interview room the detective was already sitting at the table with a recording device at his left and a computer at his right. He looked more relaxed than he had on the day of the shooting, maybe because he had been processing the crime and had made some progress toward solving it.

"Thanks for coming," the detective said. "Please have a seat. I'm sorry I kept you waiting, but I was reviewing videos from the surveillance cameras."

"Did you see anything new?" he asked, sitting down on the opposite side of the table.

"Yeah, I did. But I still haven't found what I'm looking for, so I hope you can help me find it."

"I'll try," he said.

"I'm going to record our conversation. Okay?"

"Okay." He resettled himself in the chair, trying to find a comfortable position.

"You've been staying in Westchester."

"How did you know?"

"The caller ID. You're at the guesthouse on the campus of St. Catherine College. I assume that Dr. Romero put you there."

"She's been very helpful."

"They're good people. I went to that college and got my degree in criminal justice."

"Really?"

"Yeah. Well, let's hear what you have to say."

He cleared his throat. "As you know, I was a member of Patriots for a White America. In the early spring, when people started protesting against the president, our leader organized a series of demonstrations to support him. For the next two months we travelled around the Midwest, going to cities where there were protests. When our leader heard about the protest in New York City, we took a bus from Altoona to Philadelphia, and we were driven from there to a farm in New Jersey where members of our movement were gathering. They fed us and gave us a place to sleep, in a large tent that was pitched on a pasture. They got us up at six the next morning, gave us breakfast, and brought us together for a meeting. By then there were about a hundred guys, but they weren't all members of our movement. There were Klansmen and neo-Nazis and other nutcases."

"Who brought them all together?"

"Our leader, Martin."

"Martin Stover?"

Karl nodded. "Martin wanted to unite the different white nationalist movements so they'd have more clout. The problem was, he ended up with people who had different ideas about tactics, though we all had the same goal."

"To make America white again?"

"Yeah. I wouldn't say that Martin was against violence under any circumstances, but he was generally against it. He preferred words to weapons. And he was very good with words. In fact, he talked me into joining the movement."

"I know his history. He's basically a politician."

"Anyway, after breakfast we had a meeting to discuss tactics, and that's when it became obvious that the Klansmen and the neo-Nazis had different ideas. They argued in favor of using violence, but they were outnumbered, and we finally agreed not to use violence. Most of us felt that any kind of violence would detract from our message."

"You were right about that."

"When the meeting finally ended, I was wiped out, especially after the long trip, so I wandered away from the parking lot where they held the meeting, and I went into an old barn, where I thought I'd be alone. I was sitting on a bale of hay when a Klansman came into the barn. At the meeting he'd argued in favor of violence, and he asked me how I liked the meeting. I said I didn't like meetings. He said he didn't like the way we chickened out by agreeing not to use violence. I told him it would be stupid to do anything in New York City, where they had cops all over the place. But he pulled out a gun, a German luger, and he said he was going to use it to shoot a nigger. I questioned him about that. I didn't grow up with blacks, so I had nothing against them personally, and I couldn't understand why anyone would want to kill them."

"You couldn't? But you were a member of a white nationalist movement."

"We didn't want to kill nonwhites, we only wanted to send them back where they came from."

"Okay. So this guy told you he was going to shoot a black. Did you tell your leader?"

"No, I didn't. I didn't believe he was going to do it."

"Then what happened?"

"They put us on buses and drove us into the city. I was assigned to stand in front with three other guys and deliver our message. Across the street a girl was standing, holding a sign that said LOVE WILL PREVAIL. I remember how our eyes met, and at that moment I heard the shot. A few seconds later a gun came over my head and landed on the pavement in front of me. As I told you before, I picked up the gun to prevent anyone else from using it."

"What's the name of the Klansman?"

"Junior Ritchie."

"R-i-t-c-h-i-e?"

"That's right."

He watched as Detective Ferraro keyed the name into his computer and read the results. "He's from West Virginia, and he has a record of minor infractions. If I show you some videos, could you pick him out of the crowd?

"Yeah."

"Then come around the table. We have the gun, but it was never registered to anyone, so we couldn't trace it."

"That's what he said," Karl said, getting up. He moved to the other side of the table and sat down at the left of the detective.

Together they watched a video that showed him standing in the front row across from Elsa, holding his sign, and then it showed the gun landing on the pavement. At that point the detective froze the video and called someone to join them.

A woman in uniform came into the room. She looked about Elsa's age.

"This is Sharon," the detective said. "Sharon, this is Karl."

"It's nice to meet you," the woman said politely.

"Sharon, could you show Karl the trajectory of that gun from where it landed on the pavement?"

"Sure," she said, sitting down at the right of the detective. She slid the computer toward her and started working on the keys.

They watched as the video went into reverse, with the gun rising from the pavement, going over the heads of the guys in front, and disappearing behind a sign.

"That's the problem," the detective said. "We can't see who fired the gun. Now, show Karl what the camera recorded from a few minutes earlier."

She worked on the keys, and the screen showed several guys standing around.

"Was it one of those guys?" the detective asked.

"Yeah, it's him," Karl said, pointing to a man in his mid-fifties with a low forehead and a slack jaw who stood next to the sign holder moving his mouth.

"What's he saying?" the detective asked.

"Jews will not replace us," Karl said, having heard them chant this. "Jews will not replace us."

"Great. Now, give us some pictures of him from different angles so that we can put them out."

"Sure," Sharon said. "Can I do it in the lab?"

"Yeah. But do it as quickly as possible."

Sharon left with the computer, and the detective shut off the recording device, saying: "We have enough to nail him. Of course if it goes to trial, we'll need your testimony."

"I understand. But can I leave the area now?"

"You can go anywhere. Just don't go back to those guys."

"I won't. I'll stay tonight at the guesthouse, and tomorrow I'll go home."

"You mean you'll go back to your wife and children?"

"Yeah, they're my home."

The detective nodded approvingly. "I need a number where I can reach you."

Karl gave him Linda's number because he had decided to change his number so that members of the movement couldn't reach him.

They rose from the table, and Detective Ferraro escorted him to the waiting area, where Elsa was sitting. She got up from her chair with an expectant look on her face.

"He did the right thing," the detective told her.

She hugged Karl, saying: "God bless you."

He hugged her back, remembering how a few days ago they had met on opposite sides of a street and feeling they were on the same side now.

They were able to make the 1:20 train. It was a local, with many stops, but he didn't mind. He sat at the window and gazed out at the river. Out of curiosity he started asking Elsa questions about the river, beginning with: "Where does it start?"

"Up in the mountains at Lake Tear of the Clouds."

"That sounds like an Indian name."

"It is. They were here a long time before we were. Their word for this river, Mahicantuck, means river that flows two ways."

"I don't understand."

"It's an estuary," she explained, "so a current of fresh water flows down into the ocean, and then with a change in the tide, a current of salt water flows up the river. That interflow creates an environment for a great diversity of aquatic life."

"You're talking like a professor now."

"Well, I *am* a professor," she said. "In fact, I teach a course on the Hudson River."

"We haven't talked about you much. It was always about me."

"I wasn't in trouble. You were."

"Were you ever in trouble?"

"Yeah. But someone helped me get out of it."

"Let me guess. Was it Sister Solana?"

"Yeah, it was. She saved me and became my mentor."

"How did she save you?"

"She gave me a mission to do things for others."

"What kind of things?"

"Working with kids in an after-school program, teaching English to immigrants, and providing therapy for people who can't afford it."

"What does that do for you?"

"Well, for one thing, it makes me feel good about myself."

"What else does it do?"

"It gives me ways to love people."

"What do you mean by love?"

"I mean action. Love is action, it's not a feeling."

"Did you get that from Sister Solana?"

"Yeah, I did. I got a lot of things from her."

He thought about it. "Was it her idea for you to help me?"

"It was my idea, but she joined me and took the lead."

"Okay. And what did helping me do for you?"

"It redeemed me."

"From what?"

"From hating white guys."

He laughed. "You're kidding."

"I'm not kidding. I thought I'd gotten over it, but when I saw you at the demonstration with your white skin and your blond hair and your blue eyes and your sign that said MAKE AMERICA WHITE AGAIN, it all came back. I mean, my hatred for a white guy who hurt me. So what I felt toward you wasn't love."

"What was it?"

"It was what *you* were feeling toward me."

"You mean hatred? I didn't see it in your eyes."

"I'm good at hiding what I feel."

"But if you hated me," he said after thinking about it, "then why did you want to help me?"

"I couldn't let you take the rap for killing that poor girl."

"So it wasn't love that made you want to help me?"

"It was wanting to act justly, and maybe that was a step toward love. In any case, it became love, I mean in the sense we're talking about. After being with you for a while I realized that you weren't like the guy who hurt me."

He understood. "And after being with you for a while I realized that you weren't like the immigrants who I thought were ruining our country."

They were silent for a while, and then she said: "You want to hear me talk like a professor?"

"It depends on what you're going to say."

"I'm going to say you should learn new skills so you can get a job in a different area."

"You're not talking like a professor," he said. "You're talking like my wife."

When they arrived at the Yonkers station, there were three taxis in front as well as a taxi across the street, which like the others was a Crown Victoria. He followed Elsa to the taxi at the head of the line, and they got in. The driver took them up a steep hill, passing apartment buildings that must have seen better days and then houses where the rich must have lived. They waited at a traffic light by a hospital, and then they continued to the entrance of the campus. When the driver asked Elsa where she wanted him to stop, she told him the convent. She paid him, gave him a tip, and then she composed a text message on her smartphone, presumably to Sister Solana. They stood there until she got a reply. Reading the message, she frowned in disappointment and said: "She's at San Pedro. She'll be here in a half hour."

"That's okay," he said. "Do you have to be somewhere?"

"No, I took the whole day off. I didn't know how long we'd be in the city."

"Then let's hang out until she gets here."

"Okay." She turned and headed toward the guesthouse, asking: "When are you leaving?"

"Tomorrow," he said. "Can I take a bus to St. Paul?"

"I'm sure you can. It probably leaves from Port Authority. We can check the schedule on the computer."

He used his key to open the door of the guesthouse, and he locked it behind him. They went into the kitchen, where they each got a bottle of Presidente.

"Mm, that's good," she said after taking a swig. "But it's even better on the island."

"Do you go there often?" he asked.

"We go there every other year. We still have family there."

"You mean grandparents?"

"My only grandparent lives with us here. You met her. But I have cousins and aunts and uncles there. We have a big extended family."

"That must be nice."

They had settled in the living room when there was a knock on the door.

"That must be Sister Solana," she said.

He got up and went to the door and opened it without asking who it was, and there was Junior, holding a gun on him. It was another German luger.

"Surprise, surprise," Junior said, advancing into the living room.

"How the hell did you find me?"

"It was easy," Junior said, closing the door behind him. "I heard that the cops were at the farm asking questions, and I figured they'd want to talk with you again. So I waited across the street from the precinct, and when you came out I followed you."

"The police know you killed that girl, so it won't do you any good to kill me. It'll only make things worse for you."

"If you're not around to testify, they'll never convict me."

"Yeah, they will. The police have videos of you shooting that girl. They showed them to me."

"I don't believe it. I spotted the surveillance cameras, and I hid behind a sign when I fired my gun. They only have your testimony."

"The police have a recording of his testimony," Elsa said, still holding her bottle of beer.

"Who asked you?" Junior said with a look of utter disdain for her. "It's my lucky day. I can kill another nigger."

"Don't call her that," Karl said.

"I can call her anything I want. In case you haven't noticed, I have a gun."

"If you didn't have that gun," he said, "you wouldn't last five minutes with me."

"Oh, now you're being a tough guy after being a pussy for the past few days. Well, I'm not going to give you a chance to fight with me. I'm going to kill you, and I'm going to kill your nigger, and no one will ever know who did it."

"The cops will know, and they'll catch you."

"They won't catch me if they don't know where I am."

"They'll find you," he said. "You found me, and they have more resources than you do."

"Well, you won't be around to see what happens."

Though he saw the door behind Junior opening slowly, he kept talking. "If you turn yourself in and tell the police it was an accident, you might get off lightly."

"It wasn't an accident. I meant to kill that nigger girl."

At that moment a big cop lunged into the room and grabbed Junior, with one arm wrapped around his neck and the other hand clamping the wrist of the hand that held the gun and jerking it upward. The gun fired, hitting the ceiling, and then it dropped from Junior's hand, landing on the floor. Another cop pinned Junior's arms behind him and expertly cuffed him.

After making sure that Elsa was all right—she was still sitting on the sofa, still holding the green bottle—Karl let his breath drain out in a sigh of thanks.

"Are you guys all right?" the first cop asked.

"Yeah, we're all right," he said. "How did you get here?"

"We were at the Yonkers station in a car that you probably thought was a taxi, and we saw this guy following you, so we followed him."

"But why were you there?"

"We got a call from Detective Ferraro, who thought this guy might come after you. He sent us pictures, so we had no trouble identifying him."

"Jews will not replace us," Junior started chanting.

"Yeah, yeah," the second cop told him. "Where you're going, you won't be able to wear a white hood and burn crosses."

"You have the right to remain silent," the first cop said, reading his rights to Junior.

Karl went over to Elsa, who hadn't budged. "Are you all right?"

"Yeah, I'm fine. Is that the kind of guy you hung out with?"

"Unfortunately, yeah."

The first cop made a phone call and informed the person at the other end that they had apprehended the suspect. After ending the call he said: "That was Detective Ferraro. He gave me a message for Karl. Are you Karl?"

"Yeah, I'm Karl."

"He said to have a good trip home."

"Are you from his precinct?"

"No, we're from Yonkers. Our precinct isn't far from here."

"Do you need us to go there and testify?"

"No. We saw what he was doing, and we heard what he said. He'll be tried in New York, where he killed that girl."

"Well, thanks," Karl said.

"We were just doing our job," the cop said.

At that moment Sister Solana entered the room, asking: "What happened?"

"They can tell you. It's good to see you, sister. You probably don't remember me."

"Of course I remember you," the sister said. "You're Gregory Flynn. You took my ethics course, and you had trouble with it for a while, but you finally got it."

"You're amazing, sister. That was ten years ago."

"If you'd sailed through without a problem I might not have remembered you. I don't remember every student."

"Well, it was a great course, and I learned a lot from it."

The cop said goodbye to them and joined his partner outside.

"Before you tell me what happened," the sister said, "why don't you get the Brugal. I think it might help to calm your nerves."

"Good idea," Elsa said, getting up from the sofa. She got three whiskey glasses out of a cabinet and poured doubles.

With the two women sitting on the sofa and Karl sitting in a chair, they told Sister Solana what had happened. After hearing how the police had arrived at the guesthouse just in time, she said: "*Gracias a Dios.* He was watching out for you."

They were well into the bottle of Brugal when the sister decided to order food. She called a Dominican restaurant, and she told them what to bring, including a six-pack of Presidente. It took only a half hour for the food and the beer to be delivered, and Elsa laid it out on the table: roast chicken, roast pork, fried fish, beans, rice, and fried plantains. It looked as if there was enough to feed a football team.

While they ate dinner they talked mainly about baseball, and he was surprised by how much these women knew about the sport. Between them, they knew the statistics for every Dominican player in the major leagues, and there were about two hundred of them.

Before leaving, Elsa checked the bus schedule online and found there was a bus leaving at 10:00 the next morning that would arrive in St. Paul at 4:00 the following afternoon. He told her it was fine, and she booked the trip for him, using her credit card. He asked her how much it was so that he could repay her, but she shook her head, telling him that the only repayment she wanted from him was to hear that he was reunited with his wife and children.

She said she would have driven him to the bus station at Port Authority but she had a class at nine the next morning, so she arranged to have a taxi pick him up at quarter of nine, which would give him a margin for rush-hour traffic. They agreed to meet at eight thirty the next morning so she could give him something he would need for his trip.

The next morning he was having coffee and the last piece of bread when he heard a knock on the door. Though it couldn't possibly be Junior, he jumped at the sound, and he asked who it was before opening the door.

It was Elsa with a backpack for him. "This was my brother's. He just got a new one."

"What about his clothes?" Karl said, letting her in.

"You can keep them. He doesn't need them."

He took the backpack from her and set it on the table in front of the sofa.

"Inside you'll find a toiletry bag, which could be useful."

"Man, you've thought of everything."

She stood by while he packed his clothes and toiletries as if she wanted to make sure he didn't forget anything.

He was ready to go when he heard the toot of a horn in front of the guesthouse.

"That must be Freddy," she said. "He's going to take you to Port Authority. He's a good driver."

"I bet he's Dominican."

"How did you guess?"

He went out ahead of her, and she locked the door behind them. A gray Crown Victoria was waiting in the driveway.

"Hey, professor. *Como está?*" the driver called through his open window. His smile revealed very white teeth, and his eyes were hidden by sunglasses.

"*Muy bien, y tú?*"

"I can't complain."

"Take good care of this guy," she said, handing him money.

"*Para usted yo haría cualquier cosa.*"

Karl faced her, not knowing how to express what he felt toward her, and then finally, remembering what she had said in a recent conversation, he said: "In the sense that you were talking about, I love you, Elsa."

"I love you too," she said, smiling happily. "God be with you."

They gave each other a long hug, and then he got into the taxi.

As the car moved forward he looked back and waved to her, and she waved back.

"She's a good woman," the driver said.

"Yeah, she is."

"She was my teacher in psychology, and she was the best."

"You're a student here?"

"Oh, yeah. I'm in my senior year, and I'm going to be a teacher, just like her."

"A college teacher?"

"No, a high school teacher. I majored in English."

"It wasn't your first language, was it?"

"My first language was Spanish, but I figure that after what I went through learning English, I should be able to teach it."

"Yeah. That makes sense."

As she had said, Freddy was a good driver. He navigated through the worst traffic Karl had ever seen, and he got them to Port Authority with almost twenty minutes to spare. Karl thanked him and found his way to the Greyhound station.

The bus was ready for boarding, so he got on and took a seat by the window. He leaned back and closed his eyes with an image of Elsa in his mind and a warm feeling in his heart. He was still thinking about her when the bus pulled out of its parking place. He opened his eyes while they turned and headed slowly out of the station.

As soon as they were on the road he leaned back again and closed his eyes again. The trip would take thirty hours, and all he had to do was sit there.

It happened during the second week of his senior year. He was walking down the hall with friends when he saw a girl who looked vaguely familiar but also very different. She was everything he had ever imagined in a girl, and without knowing it, she cast a total spell on him. In the class that followed he couldn't get her out of his mind, and as soon as he got home after football practice he asked his sister who the girl was.

"Describe her," Angela told him.

"She's beautiful."

"What color is her hair?"

"It's blond."

"Is it natural blond?"

"I think so. It doesn't look bleached."

"What about her eyes?"

"They're blue."

"Well, that could be a lot of girls. How tall is she?"

"She's about your height."

"It could be Linda Miller," Angela said, "but she's not new. She was a freshman last year."

"She looks vaguely familiar, but she's very different now."

"She grew up during the summer."

"That must be it. Do you know her well?"

"We're in the same homeroom."

"Do you like her?"

"Yeah. I like her a lot."

"Then why don't you bring her home sometime."

Angela laughed. "You want me to fix you up with her?"

"I just want to meet her," he said, "and I don't want to stop her in the hall."

"With all the girls who are after you, I never knew you could be so shy."

"I never felt this way before."

"Okay. I'll bring her home sometime."

It took a while, and in the meantime he was playing football, catching passes for touchdowns and being feted by everyone, including a few teachers. At the game following his conversation with his sister, he noticed Linda in the crowd for the first time. She was sitting with Angela, who must have brought her. And feeling as if he was playing for Linda, he played even harder—and dropped the ball on the next pass. At least that taught him not to pay attention to the fans.

A week later, on a Saturday afternoon, his sister brought Linda home from the movie they had gone to. He was in the yard helping his father change the screens, and seeing Linda, he almost fell off the ladder. The girls hung out in the kitchen talking, and when he was done helping his father he joined them.

His sister introduced them, saying: "Linda, this is my brother Karl."

"It's nice to meet you," he said, not knowing what else to say.

"I've seen you on the football field," she said.

"I've seen you in the hall."

There was an awkward silence, which Angela broke by saying: "Okay, you've established the fact that you've seen each other."

"I'm not much of a football fan," Linda told him. "But I did like seeing you play. You have a lot of natural grace."

"Thanks," he said. He wanted to return the compliment but he didn't know how.

"We decided to have a party," his sister said, "and if you're good, we'll invite you to it."

"What kind of party?"

"A party with music and dancing. Mom said we could have it in our basement. But she said no drinking."

"I can't drink during football season. When are you having it?"

"Next Saturday. Are you free then?"

"Yeah, I think so." He looked at Linda. "You're coming, aren't you?"

"Of course I am. I'm one of the hostesses."

The week before the party seemed longer than a month. He kept thinking about Linda and wondering if she liked him. She hadn't revealed much during their conversation in the kitchen other than that she liked seeing him play football. At least that was something, but there were probably other guys she liked to watch. There were certainly more attractive guys. And what did he have to offer a girl who was so beautiful?

There were about a dozen people at the party, about equally divided between guys and girls, including two couples who were going steady. His sister took charge of the music, which provided a background for conversations. It took him a while but he finally managed to get into a conversation with Linda in which they exchanged information about themselves and their families. He learned that her father, like his father, worked at the factory, and that her mother, unlike his mother, was a school teacher. In fact, her mother had been his teacher in elementary school, and he had liked her.

At one point his sister put on a slow, romantic ballad, and he found the courage to ask Linda to dance with him. In the darkened room they shuffled without moving across the floor, and feeling her warm body against him, and smelling her perfume, he closed his eyes and felt happier than he had ever felt in his whole life.

Linda was waiting for him at the bus station in St. Paul with Holly and Justin, who literally jumped for joy when they saw him. They rushed to him, and he put his arms around both of them at the same time, relieved that they were so glad to see him.

Linda moved toward him cautiously, checking him from head to foot as if she was afraid that he might be damaged. She finally touched his face and said: "It's good to see you."

"I've missed you," he told her.

"I've missed you too."

With the kids competing to see who would carry his backpack, he followed Linda to her car, which was parked in the lot for the bus station.

He got into the passenger seat, and the kids got in back.

"Are you home for good?" Holly asked.

"Yeah, I am," he told her with conviction. He braced himself for further questions, but there were none. He must have answered the only question that mattered to her.

"This is the downtown," Linda said as they drove through the city of St. Paul.

"It looks prosperous," he said as they passed stores that were all in business, unlike the stores in Freiburg.

"You see that building? That's where I work."

"You like your job?"

"I love it, and it pays well."

They left the downtown and went up a hill and onto an avenue that was lined with mansions. They continued on it, passing churches, and then large houses. They turned onto a side street and then onto an avenue that had smaller houses and apartment buildings. They stopped in front of a brick building, and Justin said: "This is where we live."

"It's a garden apartment," Linda told him. "We have three bedrooms, and the rent is reasonable."

"Maybe someday we'll have a house again."

"Yeah, maybe. But in the meantime this place is fine. We even have access to a yard in back, where the kids can play."

They got out of the car, with the kids competing again to see who would carry his backpack.

"It's Justin's turn now," Linda told Holly. "You carried it to the car at the bus station."

They walked to the door of the apartment, and Linda unlocked it. The kids rushed in ahead of them, and they lingered at the threshold.

"Later," Linda said, "you can tell me about your experience. But now let's go into the house and be a family. Okay?"

"Okay. I just have to tell you, I'm sorry I put you through all that shit, but it wasn't an entirely bad experience. Something good came out of it."

"I'm glad," she said. "I must say, you look a lot better than you did the last time I saw you."

"I feel better. I feel like I've been redeemed."

She scanned his face and evidently saw what she had been hoping to see, and then she put her arms around him. "Welcome home."

BOOK CLUB GUIDE

The Last Resort

Tom Milton

Introduction

Elsa Romero, a college professor, is attending a demonstration in New York City to protest the government's immigration policies. Karl Reinholdt, a white nationalist, is standing across the street from her, displaying a sign that says MAKE AMERICA WHITE AGAIN. In response she displays a sign that says LOVE WILL PREVAIL. As they stare at each other a gun is fired by someone on Karl's side, killing a girl on Elsa's side. The gun is thrown over Karl's head and lands on the pavement in front of him. Karl impulsively picks up the gun to prevent it from being used by anyone else, but the police grab him and take him away as the prime suspect. Elsa follows him to the police precinct and testifies that he didn't do it. Karl knows who did it, but out of loyalty to his movement he doesn't tell the police what he knows. Based on Elsa's testimony, the police release Karl on the condition that he remains in the area so that they can interview him further. Meeting him outside the precinct, Elsa learns that he has no place to stay and no money to pay for a hotel, and relying on her instincts, she takes him home to Yonkers where she lives with her parents.

When she introduces Karl to her parents, telling them she met him at the demonstration, they assume that he was on Elsa's side against the government, and she does nothing to correct their misimpression, not wanting to confuse them or worry them. During their conversation Karl learns that they are immigrants from the Dominican Republic, the kind of people he believes should never have been permitted to enter his country, but he has no choice but to accept their hospitality. When it's time to retire for the night Elsa takes him downstairs to a finished basement, which has a pullout bed and a full bath, and she leaves him there after getting some clean clothes from her brother, who is away for the weekend. The next morning she and her parents and her grandmother go to church in south Yonkers, where there is a ten o'clock mass in Spanish that her grandmother can understand. When they return, her mother prepares the usual Sunday dinner, and Karl learns more about the products of their home country, including coffee, beer, rum, cigars, and baseball players. That afternoon when he wakes from a siesta he receives a text message from the killer threatening him and anyone who helps him, and fearing for Elsa and her family, he tells her that he must leave them immediately.

Since he has nowhere to go, and since she believes that the only solution to his problem is for the police to catch the killer, she thinks of a place to hide him while she convinces him to tell the police who fired the gun. She calls a colleague, Sister Solana, and she determines that the guesthouse at the college is available, so she takes Karl there and introduces him to the sister, who lets them into the guesthouse and shows them around. Sister Solana is the leader of the group that participated in the demonstration yesterday, and she welcomes the opportunity to talk with someone on the other side, but she leaves them for now so that Karl can get settled in the guesthouse. Elsa makes a grocery list, which she takes to a nearby supermarket that is one of the stores in a local chain owned by her father and her uncle. Along with other essential items she brings him a six-pack of Presidente, the Dominican beer that he drank with her father, in addition to the six-pack of Bud Light that he requested. From their conversations she knows that his family has lived in Ohio for seven generations, and that being so far removed from the immigrants who were his ancestors, he feels no connection with them. Before leaving him, Elsa shows him how to use the computer so that he can learn about his ancestors and maybe realize that he has more in common with her than he thinks. But that evening Karl is happy to continue drinking Bud Light and getting his information from Fox News.

The next morning, while Elsa takes her grandmother to the eye doctor, she recalls the history of her family. Her grandmother was born on a farm in Puerto Plata Province, and she left the farm and found a job cleaning houses in the town of Santa Cruz. Her mother was born in a poor *barrio* of the town, and her mother met her father in a factory in the nearby free zone. They got married and moved into a house together in the *barrio*, where Elsa and her brother were born. The factories in the free zone closed because their foreign owners found cheaper labor in China, and the hotel where they worked for a while in menial jobs closed because a foreign company built a power plant near it, driving away the tourists with noise pollution and air pollution. The people in their *barrio* were destitute, with no jobs, no money, and no food, so her parents made the painful decision to leave their home country and come to New York. Her father found work in a bodega. Eventually her father and her uncle started their own bodega in Yonkers, and then they built a local chain of supermarkets while her parents moved from a shared apartment in Alto Manhattan to their own apartment in south Yonkers and finally to their own house in the neighborhood of St. Brigid, near the college.

Meanwhile, Sister Solana has visited the guesthouse to see how Karl is doing, and after hearing his reasons for joining a white nationalist movement, she suggests that he use the computer to do research on his ancestors, making him feel that the two women are working together in a conspiracy to convert him to their way of thinking. Still, with nothing else to do, he takes their suggestion and learns about his ancestors, who came from Germany in the middle of the nineteenth century and encountered the same kind of hostility that immigrants today are facing, even though unlike the present immigrants his ancestors were white. He is shocked to learn that people who already lived in Ohio hated the German immigrants and joined nativist movements to send them back where they had come from.

Over the next few days Karl's flashbacks reveal why he joined a white nationalist movement, and why it's so hard for him to break with it. On the other side, Elsa's flashbacks reveal why she needs to help him, and why when she faced him at the demonstration she reciprocated his feeling of hatred, even though her sign conveyed a message of love. While they meet and talk and eat meals together they believe that Karl is safe at the guesthouse, but then he receives another message from the killer who vows that he will find Karl and kill him as well as anyone who helps him, reminding them that they are still in danger.

A conversation with Tom Milton

In The Golden Door *you dealt with the issue of immigration, and in that novel you focused on how an anti-immigrant law in Alabama affected a family of illegal immigrants from Mexico who were valuable members of the community. In this novel you deal with the issue at a national level, embodied in the conflict between Karl, a white nationalist, and Elsa, a legal immigrant, who meet at a demonstration in New York City. So from the beginning we see the conflict between Karl's hatred for nonwhite immigrants and Elsa's belief that love will prevail.*

The signs they're holding tell us what their conflict is. It's a simple device, but I think it helps to get things going.

It certainly does. We know right away where they're coming from. So let's talk about Karl's hatred for nonwhite immigrants. It's not based on his personal experience, it's based on the idea that nonwhite immigrants are ruining his country. But why does he blame people who never did anything to him?

He needs to blame someone, and nonwhite immigrants are the perfect scapegoat because they're different. I mean, if people are different they stir up fear, the most primitive human emotion, and fear leads to hatred because we hate what we fear, the way children hate scary bugs.

So when politicians talk about nonwhite immigrants, they do it to arouse fear.

Arousing fear is an old political strategy. What's new is that the effects are not confined to a group of people hearing someone rant on a street corner, they go viral through social media, which are very effective in arousing fear.

The movement that Karl belongs to, Patriots for a White America, includes neo-Nazis and members of the Ku Klux Klan who have no qualms about killing people simply because they belong to another religion or race. But as I got to know Karl, I wondered why he ever got involved in such a movement.

That's a question I'm examining—why people who are fundamentally decent join such movements, and why they vote for racist leaders.

You show that Karl is fundamentally decent because when the gun that fired the shot comes over his head and lands on the pavement in front of him, he picks it up to prevent anyone else from using it. At least that's what Elsa thinks.

It's important that she thinks he picked up the gun for that reason because if she didn't, she might not trust him enough to take him home with her.

We eventually learn why Karl got involved in a white nationalist movement, but for all that has happened to him, he does have choices, and instead of doing what his wife does, he chooses to join a movement that promises to restore the world he lost. Instead of adapting to change, he resists it, and he wants to make things the way they were before.

It's a normal human tendency to resist change, but what matters ultimately is not what happens to us, it's how we deal with it. Elsa's parents had much worse things happen to them, but they adapted, and they dealt with what happened to them, whereas Karl refused to adapt, and he evaded dealing with what happened to him by joining a white nationalist movement.

Clearly, you're suggesting that a lot of people in this country have followed the route that Karl took. I mean, people who are fundamentally decent like him.

There are a lot of people like Karl in this country, and once they join a movement that promises to restore what they have lost, it's hard for them to break with the movement no matter how much it damages them.

Well, I understand what prevents Karl from breaking with the movement. It's his loyalty, and it's also his fear of losing what the movement gives him. But what exactly does it give him?

It gives him the feeling that he can keep his position as a member of the dominant group in America.

You mean white males.

That's what our current political situation is about. It's about white males trying to keep their position as the dominant group.

You make the point that Karl grew up in a virtually all-white community, where there were no immigrants, so he hates people he has never encountered. As Sister Solana says, his hatred is only in his head, not in his heart. And if it's only in his head, then the rational approach taken by the two women has a chance of working.

I think it does with people like Karl.

Do you believe he's typical of the people who join those movements?

I believe he is, but the Klansman who shoots the girl presumably grew up in a community that wasn't all-white, so his hatred is in his heart.

I understand. But you're more interested in people like Karl.

With Karl you have the possibility of change. I'm not saying you don't have a possibility with the Klansman, but I have trouble imagining Elsa and Sister Solana having any effect on him.

For the purpose of this story, the major event of Karl's life was losing his job, and you show us how devastating it was for him.

It's devastating for most people. There's no good way to lose your job, but when it happens on a massive scale as it did in his town, it destroys everyone and everything around you.

The story of this company sounds familiar. Is it based on a real situation?

It's based on a lot of situations that have occurred over the past thirty years from upstate New York to the Midwest. In cases where the jobs were outsourced to emerging countries because the labor costs were lower, we can say that the cause was globalization. In cases where the companies couldn't compete with cheap imports, we can say that the cause was foreign trade. The thing is, economists have been warning about job loss from these causes for more than fifty years, but with few exceptions, the government hasn't done anything to mitigate the damage.

How would the government mitigate the damage?

With unemployment benefits that give people enough time to learn new skills, and with training programs that teach people new skills which have market value.

How would the government pay for this?

By a tax on goods that people get at lower prices because they're coming from countries with lower labor costs.

You mean a tariff?

I mean a sales tax. The consumers who benefit from lower prices should contribute at least a portion of that benefit to people who lose their jobs because of globalization and foreign trade. That's only fair.

Do other countries do this?

They do in Europe with their value added tax.

But in the case of Karl's company the cause wasn't globalization or foreign trade, it was the debt that the private equity firms piled onto the company so they could take out their profits.

It was, and he rightfully blames them. But it's not enough for him to blame them. He needs to blame people who are more visible and more vulnerable.

Why more vulnerable?

So they can't fight back. And that's what all these movements do—they blame people who can't fight back.

It's happening in a lot of countries now.

It is, and I hope it's only a phase in a cycle, but things could get even nastier before we come around toward justice and peace.

Well, let's go back to job loss. In a scene with Karl and Sister Solana, she tells him about her own loss, and she makes him realize that while losing your job is a terrible thing, it's not as bad as losing a person you love. And she reminds him that he still has his mother and father, his sister, his wife, and his two children.

It's an indication of his mental state that he needs to be reminded of them.

But at times of loss we tend to forget our blessings, don't we?

We do. But I can tell you what my wife's father did when he lost his job. He was in his fifties, and the factory that employed him and three thousand other workers closed down and put them all out of work. At the time he had three children in Catholic schools, and the only family income was his wife's clerical salary.

What did he do?

He didn't join a white nationalist movement. He got three part-time jobs in retail, took a course in computers, and eventually got a full-time job at the data center of a large organization.

In other words, he adapted.

Instead of resisting change, he accepted it, and he fulfilled his responsibilities.

Now, what about Elsa? You wrote that when she confronts Karl at the demonstration she reciprocates his feeling of hatred. It took me a while to understand this.

It took Elsa a while to understand this. I mean to understand her motivation for helping Karl.

You mean that by helping him she redeemed herself from hating white guys.

And by letting her help him Karl redeemed himself from hating nonwhite immigrants.

Well, let's hope we find this way of redemption as a society.

Let's hope we do.

Discussion questions

1. What events changed the lives of Karl, Elsa, and Sister Solana? How did each of them deal with the event?

2. Explain Elsa's motivations for helping Karl.

3. Why is Karl willing to accept help from Elsa and Sister Solana?

4. Analyze Karl's arguments against immigration. What effect of immigration is Karl most concerned about?

5. Discuss the element of racism in anti-immigrant movements.

6. Evaluate the arguments that Elsa and Sister Solana present in favor of immigration. What is their strongest argument?

7. Compare the experiences of the immigrants in the Romero family and the Reinholdt family.

8. Explain why Karl was attracted to a white nationalist movement. In what sense did the movement provide salvation to him?

9. Analyze Karl's conflict between remaining loyal to the movement and breaking with it.

10. How do the two Dominican women help Karl break with the white nationalist movement?

11. Discuss the evolution of Karl's relationship with his wife Linda.

12. Why is Linda more willing than Karl to adapt to the changes in their world?

13. To what extent was the outcome of the story the result of the methodology used by Detective Ferraro?

14. What role does Elsa's friend Gleny play in the story?

15. Evaluate the role of white nationalist movements in the 2016 election.

16. In the context of the story, discuss the meaning of love as action, not a feeling.